Praise for Finding Balance in the Circus of Life

"*Finding Balance in the Circus of Life* was very insightful and life changing for me. It helped me to better understand who I am and what my purpose is. I understand what needs I am trying to meet. The most valuable information I learned from Carol was to live intentionally and focused and not to compare myself to others."
Dede Z. Denver, Pennsylvania

"Carol caused me to look at my role and characteristics when serving. She's real and uses humor to biblically instruct. Brilliant."
Meg N. Hatboro, Pennsylvania

"*Finding Balance in the Circus of Life* is practical and encourages women to maintain balance in their often 'crazy' lives. I especially liked the tightrope walker who reminds us to keep looking straight ahead and keep our eyes on Jesus. Using the circus to present this information is creative and enjoyable."
Carol K. Hamburg, Pennsylvania

"*Finding Balance in the Circus of Life* helped me to focus on realizing each of us can't do everything for everyone, and our job is not to please everyone. We should take our life one day at a time. We are all human, God has given us all talents; each one of these talents should be used physically and spiritually."
Jackie F. Columbia, Pennsylvania

"I LOVE this book! Carol shares inspiration and insights from God's Word as well as humorous anecdotes and examples from her own life and observations to show us how much each of us is valued and treasured by God. This book will make you think, make you laugh and, hopefully, make you want to embrace all that God has created you for!"
Cathy J. Carlisle, Pennsylvania

"Let's face it. Life is indeed a 'circus' most days. And we all need help trying to figure out our roles in the daily routine as well as in the unexpected things that happen along the way. So thankful Carol helps us identify these roles and the characteristics that define them. At some time or another we've played them all. *Finding Balance in the Circus of Life* helped me gain perspective on the delicate tightrope we do walk to find balance—something I need to acknowledge every day—and more importantly, reminded me to keep my focus on the right things to maintain that balance."
Margie M. Blandon, Pennsylvania

"Carol's approach to life's challenges is both humorous and relatable. I realize that at any point in time, even as a tightrope walker, I could lose my balance and fall! But even if I do fall, her message is clear that God is there to pick me up."
Jennie W. Stevens, Pennsylvania

"As a pastor's wife, I remember the lessons from *Finding Balance in the Circus of Life* often, especially when there seems no end to the needs of people in our church. It has shown me that I need to focus on one point and that is Jesus, because 'where the eyes look the body moves.' If I take my eyes off of Jesus I fill my life with so many nice things but not necessarily the most important. And then life gets out of balance and life gets crazy. I find that even when the wind is blowing and circumstances are difficult I won't fall off the tightrope if I'm focused on Jesus."
Carla S. Dixon, Illinois

Finding Balance
in the
Circus of Life

by

Carol R. Cool

ISBN: 978-1-63491-456-7

All Scripture quotations, unless otherwise indicated, are taken from the Holy Bible, New International Version®, NIV®. Copyright © 1973, 1978, 1984 by Biblica, Inc.® Used by permission. All rights reserved worldwide. The "NIV" and "New International Version" are trademarks registered in the United States Patent and Trademark Office by Biblica, Inc.™

Scripture quotations marked "NLT" are taken from the Holy Bible, New Living Translation, copyright ©1996, 2004, 2007, 2013, 2015 by Tyndale House Foundation. Used by permission of Tyndale House Publishers, Inc., Carol Stream, Illinois 60188. All rights reserved.

Scripture quotations marked "The Message" are taken from THE MESSAGE. Copyright © by Eugene H. Peterson 1993, 1994, 1995, 1996, 2000, 2001, 2002. Used by permission of NavPress. All rights reserved. Represented by Tyndale House Publishers, Inc.

Scripture quotations marked NASB taken from the New American Standard Bible®, Copyright © 1960, 1962, 1963, 1968, 1971, 1972, 1973, 1975, 1977, 1995 by The Lockman Foundation. Used by permission.

Printed on acid-free paper.

Cover tightrope walker illustration by Jaime Scott
Cover design by Todd Engel

Dedication—

For Les who always believes in me and
encourages me to pursue the ministry God designed me for.

DISCLAIMER

This book details the author's personal experiences with and opinions about spiritual balance and growth.

The author and publisher are providing this book and its contents on an "as is" basis and make no representations or warranties of any kind with respect to this book or its contents. The author and publisher disclaim all such representations and warranties, including for example warranties of merchantability and advice for a particular purpose. In addition, the author and publisher do not represent or warrant that the information accessible via this book is accurate, complete or current.

Except as specifically stated in this book, neither the author or publisher, nor any authors, contributors, or other representatives will be liable for damages arising out of or in connection with the use of this book. This is a comprehensive limitation of liability that applies to all damages of any kind, including (without limitation) compensatory; direct, indirect or consequential damages; loss of data, income or profit; loss of or damage to property and claims of third parties.

This book provides content related to spiritual topics. As such, use of this book implies your acceptance of this disclaimer.

Contents

Introduction:
Welcome to the Circus

"Life's a circus."

We've heard it. We've thought it. We've said it.

It's always said with a sigh, and comes out in a rush. It's become the descriptor of our lives. It conjures up the image of the old-fashioned circus. Within the big tent, different acts perform simultaneously in each of the three rings and, outside, barkers and hawkers entice you to take in a sideshow or try a new taste treat. Frenzied activity and sensory overload.

Most of us have a minimum of three rings of bustling activity operating in our lives every day. We have our home and family life. We have our work—paid or volunteer. And we have our church community.

What's odd is our circumstances don't seem to make any difference in how circus-like our lives are. Kids at home or an empty nest; working full-time, part-time, or not at all; strapped for cash or fairly flush; none of it changes the atmosphere. (Although, I'll admit, sometimes a change in circumstances does allow for more sleep.)

Life-as-circus isn't simply a product of our digital age. Bil Keane called his comic strip on domestic life *The Family Circus* at its debut in 1960—that "ideal" time period so many reminisce about. But today we believe we have more options to choose from, more hawkers begging for our time and attention.

This circus is especially chaotic because we often find ourselves orchestrating the circus while being expected to perform in all three rings at once or, at least, in quick succession. We race from one sphere to the next, changing costumes, grabbing props, and attempting to catch our breath on the run. Then we're required to clean up the resulting mess. We're also bound by our relationships to serve as spectators of the performances of others, holding our breaths when the situation gets dangerous, cheering at all the right parts.

Our lives are different from an actual circus, and potentially more dangerous to our emotional, physical, and spiritual health, because this circus of life never ends. This is no two-hour show with time to kick back and unwind afterward. The action keeps on going, with or without us, until we drop exhausted into bed at night. Often we wake up, after too little rest, feeling overwhelmed, and jumpstart our day with caffeine and multitasking, irritated we're behind before we even begin.

Is this what Jesus meant when he promised us the abundant life in John 10:10? Some Bibles read "abundantly," but the NIV has translated it as "to the full." It's full all right, overfull even. We've got so many things going on, so many opportunities to choose from, so many responsibilities to take care of, so many shoulds and coulds and oughts and musts. But is this the "full" life Jesus promised?

Is there a way to have the abundant life—a life filled with "great plenty" where I'm "amply supplied" as Merriam Webster defines abundance—that I actually enjoy? It must be possible, or God wouldn't promise it. So how do I find the balance the definition implies?

I've never been a good one for maintaining balance. On my feet, or in my life. My days are often frantic, with too much crowded in, my mind and my heart racing. My friends know I buy Eddie Bauer Balance perfume because the only way I'm getting any balance in my life most days is if I can spray it on.

Rather than wishing for a time machine to transport me to the past—whether to the romanticized past of a Jane Austen novel or the glorious days of my childhood—I wonder what steps I can take to enjoy the circus I'm living in now.

As I began to think more about an actual circus, I found some performers I could identify with and some principles I could apply to bring more balance to my days and my life. What if part of my problem is I'm taking on the role of the wrong performer? Could a particular circus performer teach me what it means to live a balanced life? I believe so.

Thanks for joining me on the journey as we take a closer look at life's circus and God's prescription for balance.

Part One:
What Kind of Performer Are You?

Have you ever taken a personality test? You know, the ones that fit you into one of four (or more) types of personalities. You might find you're a popular sanguine or a high D or the color orange or a pearl. The tests reveal your basic make-up and motivations. They show strengths and weaknesses and may tell you how to work better with others.

In the next three chapters, we are going to look at nine circus performers. Each one represents a way we might deal with our own circus of life. But they are not personalities; they are coping mechanisms. Any personality type can choose to take on one of these circus performer personas. It just might manifest itself differently.

For instance, the first performer we talk about is the ringmaster, who needs to control life. Sanguine personalities might control through their charm, while a choleric controls through her forcefulness. A melancholy uses his moodiness to control others, and a phlegmatic may choose to control through her stubbornness or lateness.

So we all—no matter our basic personality—can choose to deal with life through any of these performers' behaviors. Most of us regularly imitate one or more of the performers to manage our lives. But none of them are God's best for us. Let's take a look at why not.

Chapter 1:
The Name-Brand Performers

Our first performers are those who get the name recognition, the up-front people who attract visitors to the circus. These are the people with power, the ones who get the most money and the most face time in the media. A name-brand performer can dictate the terms; she can choose the best performing venue and nicest accommodations. These are the positions many of us want. Even if we aren't naturally aligned to these performers, we might try to "fake it till we make it," because the rewards seem worth achieving. But when we live out our daily lives using the methods of one of these circus stars, it comes with unique problems.

The Ringmaster
The ringmaster runs the circus. The whip gets cracked to keep the show moving and the performers on task. A ringmaster needs to be in control—of everything. When we become ringmasters in our world, we feel the need to tell ourselves, and everyone else, what to do, how to do it, and when.

A ringmaster finds herself running every meeting she attends, whether she's officially in charge or not. Did you ever attend a conference or meeting where you were asked to break into small groups for discussion and your first assignment was choosing a leader?

I hate that task. So much time gets eaten up in dithering. "Let's choose the person whose birthday is nearest to today," someone says. Another counters, "Maybe we should choose by ballot." The one into crafts chimes in: "I know, I'll cut up slips of paper for all of us and put a gold star on one. Whoever draws the gold star will be the leader."

By now, I'm losing control and so are other ringmaster types. "Enough already," I shout, "We're wasting time. I'll be the leader. Now, can we just get on with the questions we're supposed to discuss?" A ringmaster can't stand the lack of control, the wasted time.

As ringmasters we work at keeping our spouses and kids in line, or our coworkers. It's never an easy task. We want to make the whole circus run smoothly. We don't want surprises, and we want everything handled efficiently and according to our specifications, our desires, our plans.

Ringmasters brook no discussion. It's my way or the highway. After all, ringmasters know the best way to do everything. And seriously, ringmasters often are highly knowledgeable and efficient. They can see the big picture, everything going on in all the rings at once. But they get very frustrated when they can't control all the outcomes.

Sarah, wife of the patriarch Abraham, is a classic ringmaster. God had promised to make Abraham a great nation (Genesis 12:2). He was 75 and childless at the time—not a great start. Several years later, God visits Abraham again in a vision. By this time, Abraham is assuming his servant will inherit his property (Genesis 15:2–4). But God confirms Abraham will have a son.

And then, still no baby.

Enter Sarah the ringmaster. Abraham is 85 now, getting a little old to be procreating. Sarah figures she needs to help God out. Her clever plan is to have Abraham sleep with her servant Hagar (Genesis 16:2). After all, she figures, God told Abraham the son would be "from your own body" (Genesis 15:4), but he hadn't specifically mentioned Sarah. Maybe she wasn't part of the plan, and God was just waiting for her to figure it out.

Abraham listens to his wife. I'm sure it was a classic case of "if Mama ain't happy, ain't nobody happy." But when Hagar gets pregnant, Sarah still isn't happy. She can't control Hagar's attitude (Genesis 16:4), and things move from bad to worse. That baby, Ishmael, is the father of the Arab nations, nations still at war with Israel, the sons of Isaac. Isaac, God's promised son, didn't arrive until Abraham was 100.

Twenty-five years is a long time to wait for a promised baby, especially when the physical bits aren't working so well anymore. I understand Sarah's impatience. I've taken the ringmaster whip into my hands in much less time than 25 years.

The ringmaster, according to a Georgia Tech newsletter article, "has to shape the presentation, pace and personality of every performance while embodying the circus and the principles upon which Ringling Bros. and Barnum & Bailey has based itself on for over 130 years."[1]

When we think of the circus we call life, who should be shaping its "presentation, pace and personality"? What are the principles it should be built on? Am I capable enough to "embody" all life was created to be?

Years ago when the New Age movement was at its height, my husband Les had a t-shirt that said:

Even in this New Age, the truth remains crystal clear:

1. There is a God.
2. You're not him.

When we take on the role of ringmaster, we're trying to be God, to do his job. God should be the director of our circus, shaping its "presentation, pace and personality." He alone knows how life is meant to be lived, what he created it to be.

God doesn't want us directing our own lives or the lives of others. He wants the ringmaster position. Every Bible my parents ever gave me had Proverbs 3:5 and 6 inscribed inside the front cover. "Trust in the LORD with all your heart and lean not on your own understanding; in all your ways acknowledge him, and he will make your paths straight."

My understanding, my control, doesn't cut it. Each day I must surrender the bullhorn back into God's hands—letting him pry it away if necessary—and acknowledge his instructions and plans. He sets a pace that doesn't leave me exhausted and breathless.

And my frustration level is much lower when I recognize I'm not responsible for the actions of others in the circus. God is their ringmaster as well. If they're not measuring up, it's up to God to straighten them out, not me. I only need to be concerned with the way God wants me to live. I can find freedom in that, freedom from too much responsibility.

> **God doesn't want us directing our own lives or the lives of others.**

The Diva

There she sits, the woman in the glittery dress, riding bareback on a white stallion. All eyes are on her, marveling at her beauty. She waves a princess wave, preens a bit, draws the attention to herself. Oohs and aahs of appreciation may fill the arena as the spectators admire her sequined outfit and poise upon the horse. But too soon the elephants come clomping in or a mini car filled with clowns rolls by, and her moment in the spotlight is gone.

Divas need that spotlight. And they'll do whatever it takes to stay right in its beam.

Let's face it; many of us love being the center of attention. We may not be beauties, but we desire recognition as a star, whether for our brains, our sense of humor, our competency, our superior parenting skills, or our hard work. Are you someone who wants others to notice your efforts, to validate you with their applause? Do you live for that validation of your worth?

Actresses succumb to the allure of wanting their name up in lights on the theatre marquee, sometimes at all costs. Those marquees were nicknamed "electric tiaras" by theatre historian Ben Hall. He was referring to their shape and the flashing lights that glittered like diamonds. But I think it a fitting description of what they did for the performers whose names appeared in lights as well. The "electric tiara" crowned the theatre diva as worthy of accolades, attention, and adoration.

The problem is, attention is fleeting. A diva is only as good as her last show. As soon as she has an off day, the wolves circle, ready to pick her off. The fans move on to the next rising star. And it doesn't even take failure. Like the diva on the stallion, we can't hold the attention or applause of others forever. Something new, something louder, something funnier, will soon come behind us and draw their eyes away from us.

In Helen Fielding's book *Olivia Joules and the Overactive Imagination*, Olivia, the main character, has 16 rules for living. Number two is "No one is thinking about you. They're thinking about themselves; just like you." That explains why it's often so hard to remember the name of the person we've just been introduced to. We weren't thinking about them. We were thinking about what they might be thinking of us.

We're selfish creatures. All of us. It makes it hard for the diva to ever get enough attention. She's always trying one more stunt, one more push for perfection, to capture just a few more minutes of fame. But it never lasts.

The book of Acts doesn't tell us much about the life of Sapphira, but I'm willing to bet she was a diva. Sapphira and her husband Ananias see Barnabas sell some land and give the money to the fledgling church. You have to imagine people were pretty impressed by this generous gift. Barnabas was probably given all sorts of praise for his selfless act.

Sapphira and Ananias want in on the action (Acts 5). We don't know if their intentions were always warped or if they started out with a sincere desire to give generously. All we know is once they sold the property, they decided to keep some of the money for themselves. This wasn't a problem; all of it was theirs to begin with. What was wrong was they decided to pretend they were giving the church all the money from the sale. They wanted to appear as generous as Barnabas—with a bit less pain.

Here's where it gets interesting and I believe we see Diva Sapphira. Ananias comes alone to present the gift to the church. Sapphira doesn't show up until three hours later. Why? I think they figured they could both get praised separately, twice the accolades, if they came at different times.

Now you might think the true diva would have gone first, taking Ananias's place. But I think Sapphira knew once Ananias presented their gift, people would go off and tell their friends. An even bigger crowd would be gathered by the time she arrived to get her glory.

When we pursue the glory meant for God, we end up desperate.

Maybe she got her bigger crowd, but Sapphira didn't get the glory she was after. She was getting the news her husband had been struck dead because he'd agreed "to test the Spirit of the Lord" (Acts 5:9). And then Peter tells her she's going to die immediately as well. Not a great day for a diva.

God's ideal for us isn't the pursuit of personal glory. He created us wonderfully, but not so we can receive the glory. In Isaiah 42:8, he says, "I am the LORD; that is my name! I will not give my glory to another." We will never be satisfied when we're seeking glory for ourselves because glory doesn't belong to us.

When we pursue the glory meant for God, we end up desperate. We resemble the too-old former bombshell dressed in inappropriate clothing with make-up applied with a trowel. People are embarrassed by our neediness and turn away. And we get even less of the appropriate kind of attention.

We resent the person who's now the darling, the person the crowds admire and want to get close to. We get snarky, trying to bring her down. We trust no one and no one trusts us, and we're lonelier still.

God wants our lives to have purpose for his kingdom. As we fulfill that purpose we find satisfaction in being part of God's plan. It's a joy that doesn't rely on the attention or praise of others. It's the joy of knowing God is pleased with our actions and attitudes, and we're drawing attention to him and his kingdom. And best of all, we find ourselves as part of a community, working together for God's glory.

The Lion Tamer

"Lord of the Rings ... King of the Jungle ... The Golden Gladiator ... Caesar of the Circus!"[2] That's how the program book for the 119th edition of "The Greatest Show On Earth" described Gunther Gebel-Williams, Ringling's famous lion tamer. In 1968, Irvin Feld, then owner of the Ringling Bros. and Barnum & Bailey Circus, bought the entire European circus Gebel-Williams worked in to get this extraordinary performer as part of his show.

We question the sanity of a lion tamer for his willingness to enter a cage with lions and tigers, to open a lion's mouth and stick his head inside. Yet we can't pull our eyes away. Gebel-Williams was said to have "captured the imagination of the American public with his dashing style and daring performances."

It's this daring that drives the lion tamer. They live for the excitement, the adrenaline rush. They need adventure. And lest life get too boring, they're constantly adding another layer of danger. It was true for Gebel-Williams, according to the Ringling program book: "Each season [Gebel-Williams] created new and more sensational acts, each one topping the last."

Having a love of adventure, like the lion tamer, can bring joy to our lives and open up new opportunities. I love traveling, discovering the tastes and vistas around the world. I love exploring new things, eating something I've never eaten before. But sometimes our hunger for adventure can put us in danger.

It might not be dangerous in the same way as when Gebel-Williams "brought together 15 leopards, three panthers and two pumas in the same cage [and then] lay down among them as they swarmed over his body." That's just nuts.

But our constant need for adventure can bring dissatisfaction with life as it is, even as it was meant to be.

When our daughter was growing up, we knew a woman I'll call Collette, who had been divorced multiple times. Somewhere around the three-year mark of each marriage, Collette would declare her husband inadequate, unsuitable. She would leave him, but she always had another man waiting in the wings.

Our astute 15-year-old said one day, "Collette is in love with love, isn't she?" Exactly. She loved the thrill, the adventure, of falling in love. When life evened out, when it got boring—with laundry to do and dishes to wash, with a fallible human being sitting on the sofa—she bailed. Off she went looking for the next thrill.

People who suffer from addictions to gambling or drugs or money or shopping are also lion-tamers. They're always looking for the next high, all the while sure they can control the beast they've allowed into their lives. But often the beast turns on them, overpowering them, leaving them battered and broken or in debt.

Samson was a lion tamer—quite literally, according to Judges 14:5–6, where it tells us he met a lion and tore it apart with his bare hands. That lion was tamed permanently.

But he was also a figurative lion tamer. He pursued women who weren't Israelites, against God's commandments. He let those women play games with him, begging and wheedling to find out the secret of his strength. He kept at it even though he had to know Delilah was trying to destroy his strength because she put in place every ploy he said would make him weak (Judges 16). Maybe he believed he could control her. He seemed to think it was all a game, until a shave did him in. He'd provoked the Philistines through riddles and strange killings. But then he pursued one thrill too many and was defeated.

When we play with fire, we eventually get burned. If we walk too close to the mountain edge, one day our feet slip and we tumble to our deaths. For 13 years, performers Siegfried and Roy performed with white tigers and lions. They did more than 5,000 shows. But one day the thrill seeking brought a near-death experience. A tiger grabbed Roy by the neck and mauled him. He never fully recovered.

Often we don't either when we pursue the thrill instead of God's will. What we're pursuing may not be wrong in and of itself. But how we pursue it can still be wrong. My travel bug can be harmful if it leads me into debt or to sacrifice responsibilities in pursuit of the next good meal or the most fascinating ruin. Envy creeps into my life and eats at my heart as I think of our friend Nathan who has visited all seven continents and manages regular trips abroad.

Paul warns against the subtle power of pursuing pleasure in Titus 3:3 (NASB), reminding us it should stay as part of our pre-Christ life. "For we also once were foolish ourselves, disobedient, deceived, enslaved to various lusts and pleasures, spending our life in malice and envy." Instead he tells us in verse eight to "be careful to engage in good deeds."

Living a life for Christ, filled with good deeds, is its own adventure. God provides amazing opportunities, some even fraught with danger. But it's not foolish, as Paul calls the pursuit of pleasure in Titus. It's adventure and danger with a goal bigger than the rush of adrenaline or the accolades of men. It's an adventure that brings the joy of fulfilling the purpose God designed for us.

Questions for Contemplation or Discussion

1. How do you see yourself taking on the persona of one of these name-brand performers?

2. Why do you think it's so easy for you to perform in that act?

3. What benefits does that performance bring to your life?

4. What negative impact does that performance have on your life?

5. Do you think other people influence you to perform in a certain act?

6. Does being a Christian make you feel you should perform in one of these acts?

7. What guilt do you find in your life based on the act(s) you are (or are not) part of?

Chapter 2:
The Nuts-and-Bolts Performers

When we think of the circus, we immediately think of these essential performers. We can't imagine it being a circus without them. What circus doesn't have clowns? And the jugglers and trapeze artists do the heavy lifting of entertaining the crowds. These are the people who get the job done. The church needs people who get the job done as well. After all, jobs abound. But when we live to take on one of these roles—at home, at work, at church or in our community—we may not be focusing on the right things.

The Clown

What is the role of the circus clown? That's easy—to make people happy. Bruce Johnson, a.k.a. Charlie the Juggling Clown, says, "A clown performs for the enjoyment of others. ... They try to make others happy and feel good about themselves."[3]

Clowns live only for the happiness of others. They go to extreme lengths to do so. Remember those clowns at the circus stuffing themselves into mini-cars? Their sole purpose is to bring pleasure to others, to ensure they have a good time. What's wrong with that? We all love people who make us laugh, who make us happy. And if that's their main goal in life, all the better for us.

But is someone else responsible for my happiness? Or is the clown in the circus of life taking on a responsibility God never meant for him or her to have?

In our house, we have another name for the clown persona—we call it the cruise director. The cruise director not only plans all the entertainment for the passengers but also handles any problems that arise and affect passenger happiness. I've never been on a cruise, so my cruise director picture comes from 1970s and '80s TV. Yes, the smiling Julie McCoy on *The Love Boat,* graciously handling complaints and providing experiences to make sure the cruise was memorable for those on board.

Years ago, we took a group from our church on a trip to an Amish grocery story we frequented. The store was an hour away but boasted tremendous bargains that, for my husband and me, made it worth the trip. We had talked it up to the others, and they were eager to score some bargains for themselves.

Once we arrived, families grabbed their carts and headed on out. My husband Les is our primary cook, so he makes the majority of the food choices, but I normally shop with him.

Not this day, however. I kept wandering the aisles, homing in on our group members. "How's it going? Are you finding good bargains? Do they have stuff you want? Are you glad you came?"

Finally, my best friend stopped me. "Carol, their happiness is not your responsibility. They chose to come along. You are not the cruise director. Now, go back to your cart." Humbly, I did.

But playing cruise director or clown, taking on the responsibility for someone (or everyone!) else's happiness, is a habit that dies hard with me. Once my friend Cyndi who lived an hour and a half away begged me to come out and help her find a new church. We visited a church we had heard good things about. We arrived while Sunday school was still in session. As we read the bulletin, we noticed it mentioned all the adults would have Sunday school together in the sanctuary for a seminar entitled, "How to be a welcoming church."

"Oh, no," I said to Cyndi, who doesn't like crowds, "Those doors are going to open and people are going to swarm out of there and mob us after that lesson." We braced ourselves.

The doors opened. Everyone poured out. Not a soul spoke to us.

We went inside and sat down. We sat in the pew, ignored by the people entering around us. I noticed another woman seated alone on the other side of the auditorium. After a while, I felt so badly for her, I couldn't help myself. I walked over and asked if she'd like to join us. Turned out she was waiting for a friend. The cruise director slunk back to her seat.

Les and I have now developed a code phrase when I get like this: NMP. It stands for Not My Problem. I am not required to make everyone happy, to solve every uncomfortable situation.

The sad part about being a clown is your own self worth depends on the response of others. You are only valuable, in your own mind, if others respond well to your work, your efforts. If you can make them happy, then you feel fulfilled.

This leaves you at the mercy of the whims of others. Some people will never be happy, no matter how hard you try to please them. But if being a clown is the persona you've adopted in life, you'll simply keep trying, over and over again. Others maintain a power over you and may even be aware of it and enjoy it. A woman who remains in an abusive relationship, making excuses for a husband who belittles or batters her and believing she's at fault for not making him happy, is the extreme example of clown thinking.

The sad part about being a clown is your own self worth depends on the response of others.

Jacob's unwanted wife, Leah, is a sad example of this clown behavior and the pain it can bring to person's life. In Genesis 29 verse 31, it says, "When the Lord saw that Leah was not loved, he opened her womb." God gives Leah a child because her husband doesn't love her. Leah acknowledges this in choosing to name her son Reuben, which means, "See, a son." She's hopeful bearing a son for Jacob will improve their relationship, will make him happy with her. After naming him she says, "Surely my husband will love me now."

But he doesn't. The second son comes, Simeon, whose name means "one who hears," because she knew God heard she wasn't loved. But we find no change in Jacob's attitude.

Son number three arrives and she names him Levi, which means "attached," saying, "Now at last my husband will become attached to me." But she's wrong. Even after a fourth son, Jacob is still not delighted with her. She becomes so desperate she follows her sister Rachel's example by insisting Jacob sleep with her servant girl so she can claim the children as her own.

After some bargaining with Rachel, Jacob's favored wife, Leah gets Jacob back in her bed. She bears him two more sons, Issachar and Zebulun. We see Leah's goal in all of this is still one thing: to make Jacob happy, to have him love her. She names the last son Zebulun, which means "honor," and says, "This time my husband will treat me with honor."

And that expresses the truth of a clown's desperate push to make others happy. By making them happy, we achieve worth. It's Sally Field at the Oscars, shouting, "I can't deny the fact that you like me, right now, you like me!" The phrase "right now" is telling—people change and when we base our worth on their opinions of us, we'll always be on edge, always doing whatever it takes to make them happy so they like us.

God wants us to find our worth in him. We are his workmanship, Ephesians 2:10 tells us, and he gives glory and honor to us as his creation (Psalm 8:5). Doing nice things for others isn't wrong, nor is wanting to contribute to their happiness, but it can't be the focus of our lives. Our focus needs to be on living to please God, and then we won't be ruled by the opinions of others.

The Trapeze Artist

"He'd fly through the air with the greatest of ease, that daring young man on the flying trapeze." I remember that song from my childhood, so I was surprised to learn it was written in the mid-1800s about a specific trapeze artist named Jules Léotard. (And yes, the leotard was named after him.) Léotard was the first performer known for "flying" from one trapeze to another and for performing a somersault in the air.

Trapeze artists swing from one side of the circus to the other in a great arc. This is one circus performance we think we understand a bit, thanks to those years on the grade school swings. We know the thrill of soaring up, that moment of suspension at the apex before we come hurtling back down. Suddenly we're on our way back up again, only on the other side.

My husband Les hates it when I read any books or articles in the how-to or self-help categories. He knows I'm sure to adopt whatever great advice I come across. I launch myself into it with gusto—for a few moments or days at least. Then I bore of it and come swinging down, just before sailing up to the next great self-improvement project. Like Jules Léotard, sometimes I even launch myself from one crazy idea to another, flying through the air without even a moment of normal life.

When we live our daily lives as a trapeze artist, we're busy swinging from one extreme to another with no lasting focus. We might have a single moment of suspension where we're "all in" to whatever idea has caught our fancy, but it doesn't last long. Soon we've left it behind, headed back to earth. But we don't stay down for long. We immediately swing away toward a different extreme, some new interest.

These extremes waste three of our most limited personal resources: time, energy, and money. I saw a magnet once that said, "I went on a special 21-day diet. All I lost was three weeks." When I pick up some new improvement scheme, I may buy new foods or household products. I may throw out those clothes that don't project the new me. When I bore of the scheme, the new juicer ends up in a bottom cupboard, the foods rot in the veggie drawer, and I wonder if I can buy my comfortable pants back from Goodwill.

We have so many options to choose from in life. It can be hard to focus on one or two things, to stick with them, and to do them well. Part of the problem is the articles and books make it seem so easy. "Five Simple Steps for Making Your Own Potpourri" says the headline, and we believe it's that simple. At least until we get started.

Once, when I was trying to save money, a book promised me I could make my own liquid soap. All I needed to do was buy glycerin. I searched and found it, spent money on it, and took the time to make my own soap. I proudly poured it into all my liquid soap dispensers.

The concoction soon hardened up inside each one, clogging the nozzles and dispensing no soap, liquid or otherwise. I had to replace all four of my soap dispensers and the soap. Not such a money-saving venture after all.

The diet advice or home organizing advice might work if we just stuck with it, but soon another article offers a better or faster or less painful way to do it. So we abandon plan A and move on to plan B. We want good results but not at any personal cost. We don't want it to take our time or energy or effort to achieve. We want instant results, microwaveable remedies. All gain, no pain.

Life doesn't work like that, no matter what the supermarket checkout line headlines say.

Tucked into the books of the Minor Prophets in the Old Testament is the strange and heartbreaking story of Hosea. Have you ever noticed God gives his prophets some really strange tasks? Simple, easy five-step plans are strangely absent.

You've got Jeremiah being instructed to make a yoke for his own neck and to wear it while giving the king God's message that they'd be enslaved (Jeremiah 27:2–8). Ezekiel was told to draw the city of Jerusalem in clay and build little siege works against it. Then he had to lie beside it for 430 days and use his own excrement as fuel for his cooking fire. When Ezekiel protests he doesn't want to defile himself by cooking over human excrement, God allows him to use cow manure instead (Ezekiel 4:1–15). Wow, so much better!

Hosea, though, gets no reprieve from defilement. His instruction is the strangest to me because it ties up his heart and emotions, not just his body. "When the Lord began to speak through Hosea, the Lord said to him, 'Go, take to yourself an adulterous wife and children of unfaithfulness, because the land is guilty of the vilest adultery in departing from the Lord.' So he married Gomer" (Hosea 1:2–3a).

Gomer is a trapeze artist. She's a prostitute, flying from one man to another. But Hosea marries her at God's command. She's with him long enough to father two sons, but then, at some point, she defects, soaring back into the arms of other men. Maybe life as the preacher's wife is too hard. Maybe she wants the goodies and excitement these men provide her (Hosea 2:4). She considers returning to her husband when life gets rough (Hosea 2:7), but Hosea has to actually buy her back again, probably from her pimp.

Gomer wanted the new, the exciting, the alluring, the easy way. She wouldn't stick with one man, one life. As soon as life got hard, she packed up and moved on.

Les and I were young when we got married, and I was starry-eyed. I thought we agreed about everything, big and little. Yeah, you've been there. Reality hits, whether it's the way someone squeezes the toothpaste tube or the way they chew or how they deal with their dirty clothes. Suddenly we realize this marriage thing takes work, and we wish for the easier path, the one where what we want wins without any sacrifice on our part. But if we bail, we miss out on the end product, in this case, a satisfying lifelong marriage.

New isn't always bad. New methods, new ideas, new plans can bring us new hope. And certainly God does new things in his church and in the lives of his people. "See, I am doing a new thing! Now it springs up; do you not perceive it?" God says in Isaiah 43:19. When he's bringing something new into our lives, he wants us to recognize it. But that doesn't mean it will be easy. His way often requires hard work. He doesn't want us to pursue the new simply because it seems like a faster way to get results, abandoning the work he called us to do in pursuit of the shortcut.

The trapeze life has no lasting focus. We swing back and forth, enjoying higher arcs or a farther leap to a new trapeze altogether. But nothing permanent is accomplished in our lives. Like those days on the grade school swings, we often reach the point where we're dizzy and sick, needing to get back down to earth as quickly as possible.

The Juggler

Jugglers fascinate us. We're mesmerized by the balls or clubs or swords or even chainsaws spinning through the air. We wait for the juggler to miss. And we wonder, could I ever do that? Who hasn't attempted to juggle at least two balls to see if you can get the rhythm down?

And while physical juggling may have never worked out well for us, in our society we've all become pretty adept jugglers of tasks. The problem is we don't know when to quit. We're always adding another plate or ball to our already overfilled hands.

Do you have trouble saying, "No"? We believe we can multitask, but if the truth is told, I'm not a proficient juggler. It seems I'm always dropping something. An article in *TIME* magazine called "Staying Sharp" had this to say about multitasking: "A long history of psychological research has proved what one might expect: performance declines—and stress rises—with the number of tasks juggled."[4] Our juggling stresses us out, and what we're doing isn't done as well as it would be if we did one thing at a time.

Our juggling stresses us out, and what we're doing isn't done as well as it would be if we did one thing at a time.

Massachusetts' psychiatrist Edward Hallowell has even invented a new word—frazzing—to describe this phenomenon. Frazzing is "frantic, ineffective multitasking, typically with the delusion that you are getting a lot done. The quality of the work, however, is poor."[5] Did you catch that word "delusion"? Most of the time we're kidding ourselves about our productivity.

Back in 2005 a British study found, "The distractions of constant emails, text and phone messages are a greater threat to IQ and concentration than taking cannabis."[6] The average IQ loss was 10 points, more than double that of pot smokers! Imagine what the studies would reveal today when all of these technologies have become so pervasive.

It's hard to imagine our lives without multitasking. We've done it for as long as we can remember. Most women believe they couldn't get through life without juggling.

And apparently we have a long history of it. The earliest record of juggling comes from drawings on the walls of the tomb of Baqet III, an Egyptian provincial governor, from about 2,000 BC. His tomb is number 15 found in the village of Beni Hasan. Several women are pictured juggling balls.[7]

In the Bible we find a juggler by the name of Martha. She wasn't juggling balls; she was juggling tasks, much like her female counterparts today. Jesus has come for a visit, along with his disciples. Martha is attempting to juggle all the work necessary to feed this houseful. Luke 10:40 describes her state of mind: "But Martha was distracted by all the preparations that had to be made." It wouldn't be easy to feed an extra thirteen people in that era. No Stove Top Stuffing Mix existed to whip up and stretch the meat, no frozen veggies to drop in a pan of boiling water. Martha had a lot to do, so much so it distracted her.

What did it distract her from? Spending time with Jesus. That's where her sister Mary was. She's described in the same verse as sitting "at the Lord's feet listening to what he said." Does Mary remember a baker's dozen of men might be hungry? We don't know, but Jesus commends her for choosing "what is better" (verse 41).

Like most of us when we multitask, Martha gets irritable when it doesn't all work out. (Which it rarely does.) She appears before Jesus demanding he order Mary to multitask too. "Lord, don't you care that my sister has left me to do the work by myself? Tell her to help me!" (verse 40).

I can picture Jesus shaking his head sadly, as he says: "Martha, Martha, you are worried and upset about many things, but only one thing is needed." He then tells her the needed thing is the one Mary has chosen to do, to sit and listen to him.

We have no record of what happens next. Did Martha sit down and forget about dinner? If that were so, did the disciples and Jesus ever get fed at all? Or did Martha stalk back to the kitchen muttering under her breath, "Men, what do they know about all the work it takes to get a meal together. Sure, sit at your feet. Let's see who's squawking later when you're hungry and no supper is ready."

My reaction is often filled with sarcasm when someone suggests I'd do better to give up the juggling and tackle one task at a time. But the studies all seem to suggest they're right. Can we trust God to give us the time and energy to do what he's called us to, one task at a time, and learn to disregard the rest?

Questions for Contemplation or Discussion

1. How do you see yourself taking on the persona of one of these nuts-and-bolts performers?

2. Why do you think it's so easy for you to perform in that act?

3. What benefits does that performance bring to your life?

4. What negative impact does that performance have on your life?

5. Do you think other people influence you to perform in a certain act?

6. Does being a Christian make you feel you should perform in one of these acts?

7. What guilt do you find in your life based on the act(s) you are (or are not) part of?

Chapter 3:
The Nonperformers

Like any successful organization, the circus doesn't run without those who operate behind the scenes, those who enable the performers to do their jobs and live in the spotlight. These people usually work unnoticed, but if they chose not to show up for work, the whole production would quickly unravel. In the church and in business, we need people who are willing to work behind the scenes, smoothing the way for others, handling the tasks others don't even notice. But some of us take refuge in these roles, not because God has called us to them, but because we're too fearful of doing the work God created us for.

The Spectator

No circus would be complete without the spectator, cheering in the stands, laughing at the clowns, buying the popcorn. Spectators are content to let others work while they're entertained. I once had a T-shirt that said, "Work fascinates me; I could sit and watch it for hours." And many of us are satisfied to live right there. We play armchair quarterback, happy to sit back and be entertained while we critique the show (a nice way to say "criticize"). It's so much easier to know the best way to have done something if we aren't the ones who actually have to do it.

A recent broadcast of ESPN's *Monday Night Football* had almost 16 million viewers. While 22 men battle it out for the win, millions look on. Even if you count the full roster of dressed players, 46 on each team, each man playing the game represents 172,000 others who have found a comfortable seat and settled in to act as critic. We find ourselves disgusted at a badly executed play, shouting advice to a coach who can't hear us and wouldn't take our advice if he did. (But we know the team would have performed better if he'd listened to our wisdom.) We become so engrossed in the game, so identified with "our" team, that when they win, we feel we've achieved something great, even though the only time we left the recliner was to grab a bag of chips.

As spectators, we may even begin to enjoy looking for the mistakes of others. I am pretty certain this is why reality TV shows like *American Idol* often include one or two people at the start who just can't sing. We laugh at their attempts, at their ludicrous belief they could make it as a pop star with that voice. We feel so superior, and yet we've attempted nothing.

I've noticed over the years those most critical of their local church are those who are doing the least. They sit back in their comfortable pew and tell the other spectators what a poor job the pastor did with his sermon, or how the choir was off-key, or why the children aren't learning in Sunday school. Things would run better if the board would just listen to their advice. But they never lift a finger to help. When the church asks for volunteers for a ministry or a board position, they fold their arms and then show disdain for what they perceive are a lack of qualifications in those who take up the challenge and do the job.

> **When we're part of the team, on the field, we're much less likely to criticize.**

When we're part of the team, on the field, we're much less likely to criticize. We're too busy doing, trying to be part of the solution, attempting to achieve great things. We're focused on our part of the task, recognizing the need to encourage others on the field so we can all work together to accomplish the goal.

If you find yourself being critical at church or within a club or organization, ask yourself if you're actually playing the game or if you're sitting in the cushy club box, watching the action from above.

Get on the field. You'll be surprised what you discover about the challenges and intricacies of the game plan when you're on the team working to execute it.

I've been part of a women's club for the several years, and about two years in I realized I'd become disillusioned with the leadership and was sniping to other members about their way of leading. As I thought about this spectator mentality, I decided it was time to shut up and step up. I chose to join the board as the programming chair.

What I discovered in that year was keeping the club running took far more work than I realized and required the energy of many people. By choosing to become part of the solution, I helped the club, but more importantly, I learned to resist judging the efforts of others. Now I know the personal cost and the work involved, and I'm much more of a cheerleader for those who choose to lead.

Michal was the first wife of David, the Goliath killer. A daughter of King Saul, she loved David (1 Samuel 18:20) and Saul married her off to him. When her father threatens to kill David in a jealous fit of rage, Michal plots a way for David to escape and lies to cover up her part in scheme (1 Samuel 19:11–17). She certainly wasn't a spectator then.

But while David is in his years of wilderness living, hiding from Saul, Michal is married off to another man. When David becomes king after Saul's death, he demands Michal be given back to him even though he has several wives now.

I don't think it was a happy marriage anymore. Maybe Michal had fallen in love with her second husband Paltiel. He had certainly loved her, for he followed her weeping as she was returned to David (2 Samuel 3:14–16).

We only hear from Michal one more time and by then she has become a classic spectator. The ark of the covenant had been captured by the Philistines during her father's reign. God had punished the Philistines for keeping the ark and so they had returned it to Israel. It ended up in the town of Kiriath Jearim for 20 years (1 Samuel 7:2).

David decides he wants to bring it to Jerusalem, but he doesn't have it transported the way God prescribed. They put the ark on an oxen cart and when the cart hits a bump, Uzzah the priest reaches out his hand to steady the ark. Touching the ark is a big no-no. Uzzah dies because of it. Everyone is frightened, David is angry, and the ark is left at the house of Obed-edom (2 Samuel 6:1–10).

When David hears that Obed-edom is being blessed by God because the ark is at his house, he decides again to bring the ark to Jerusalem. This time he transports it correctly. "The entire house of Israel" went with David to worship God and celebrate the ark's return (2 Samuel 6:15). Everyone except Michal, that is.

Michal stays home, watching from the window. What she sees is her husband, the king, wearing a simple linen robe and dancing his heart out before God. He leaps and he dances, praising God. And Michal is "filled with contempt for him" (2 Samuel 6:16, NLT).

David comes home filled with joy, ready to bless his house, and Michal rains on his parade: "How distinguished the king of Israel looked today, shamelessly exposing himself to the servant girls like any vulgar person might do" (2 Samuel 6:20, NLT). She is more concerned about his status, about him looking right, than she is about him doing the right thing before God.

She didn't even bother to join the procession, but she knows best what it should have been like. And it certainly shouldn't have included the king making a fool of himself. A true spectator, Michal chooses to criticize.

David's response is beautiful: "I was dancing before the Lord … I celebrate before the Lord. Yes, and I am willing to look even more foolish than this, even to be humiliated in my own eyes! But those servant girls you mentioned will indeed think I am distinguished" (2 Samuel 6:21–22, NLT). David was only concerned about honoring God.

The final verse of the chapter is, to me, one of the saddest in Scripture. "So Michal, the daughter of Saul, remained childless throughout her entire life" (2 Samuel 6:23, NLT). It doesn't say that God punished her for her scorn and criticism and closed her womb. Perhaps David never slept with her again. Whatever the cause, in a day when a woman's worth was often determined by her ability to produce children, this was devastating. Her value was gone. And we never hear mention of her again.

Perhaps Michal was tired of her life. She loved David. But he becomes a fugitive and she's married off to another. And then she's dragged back to David as one of his many wives. Her emotions have been through the wringer. And so she turns bitter. She sits back as a spectator.

Sometimes we, too, become spectators because we're tired of it all. We've been in the game, and we've gotten hurt. Maybe it was our own fault, maybe an accident, or maybe we were even targeted by another player. Sometimes we need to take a step back to find healing.

But quitting the game is different from sitting on the bench for a while. An injured player who sits on the bench knows she's part of the team. Her mind is still engaged in the game, even if she can't play. She's rooting for her teammates, not badmouthing them.

Hannah, a young woman from our church, loved playing high school sports. She was a setter/weak side hitter on the volleyball team and a power forward on the basketball team. Unfortunately, she tore her ACL, PCL, and lateral and menial menisci the summer between her freshman and sophomore years and that August had surgery to repair the extensive damage.

She continued on for one more season as the volleyball manager. She took stats and went to every practice and game that she was physically able to after the surgery. The head basketball coach didn't want Hannah to simply be a manager. He made sure she knew she was a team member, and his approach helped her mindset.

During her sophomore year Hannah attended basketball camp on crutches, just to sit there. She went to every practice and every game. Her coaches named her the JV captain, and she was assigned to "coach" a few younger players to help them develop their game. She became a better student of the game as she sat on the bench.

When she reinjured her knee in her senior year, she again worked on training the younger girls. She was a captain and took the leadership role very seriously. She missed just a few practices that year because of her second surgery, but still attended every game, even though she would never be well enough to again play high school basketball.

If we need time to heal—spiritually, emotionally or physically—we may need to sit out a game or two or even a season, but we're still part of the team. Like Hannah, we have to be present when possible, encouraging those in the game, not wallowing in self-pity, and certainly not criticizing those who are on the field.

I've learned to check myself—my attitudes, my emotions, and my willingness to be part of the solution. I'm full of good ideas for any organization I'm a part of. But I often don't want to do the work to execute them. I want to dream them up and then watch others do the hard work to bring them to fruition. I could watch others work for hours. But God wants me in the game.

The Go-Fer

The go-fer is vital to all the circus performers. I'm not talking about the animal—the gopher—but rather the one who must "go-fer" stuff. She runs and fetches the missing prop or piece of apparel or goes for the special treat the name-brand performer craves. "Be a good girl and grab me a _____ " is the request she hears 50 times a day. And she does. She caters to the whims of the rest of the performers.

Helping others is good; the rest of the performers rely on the go-fer and can't imagine how they'd survive without her. But the go-fer is so busy helping others fulfill their destiny she never gets into her own act. The go-fer has the need to provide for everyone else and doesn't often think about her own dreams or what God might have created her to do.

The go-fer life is prevalent in the church. We see it especially in women, this almost desperate need to be the "good girl," which is perceived as the "godly girl." She fills her days meeting everyone else's expectations, but she's never doing what she's called to do. The go-fer—the good girl—is loved by everyone, because she rarely says no, especially if you frame the request right.

When I was a teen we had a youth pastor who would walk up to people, put his arm around their shoulders, point off into the distance and say: "Picture Jesus dying on the cross for you. Do you see it? Do you see him bleeding and suffering for you?" After a pause for you to gulp and nod your head yes, he'd move in for the kill: "Now don't you want to do something for him?"

That kind of reasoning is hard for the go-fer to resist. Whatever the job someone asks us to do, as long as it's for Jesus, we feel the need to step in and take it on. A person who has the spiritual gift of helps or service is most susceptible. After all, he or she reasons, God gave me this gift of helping others; therefore I have to use it. I must take on this task.

But a need does not constitute a call from God. You'll always find a plethora of needs, places you can serve, ministries you can give to, jobs to be filled. God never expected you to fill them all. It's impossible. But it doesn't stop the go-fer from trying.

A need does not constitute a call from God.

Because the go-fer always says yes, the word gets around. More and more people ask her to do things. "Ask so-and-so. She's always a willing volunteer." Requests bloom like dandelions in the spring. Each yes the go-fer says serves as the puff of breath sending the dandelion seed off to proliferate. More requests arrive.

One of the young women in our church years ago had the gift of helps. Whatever needed doing, she did. Need a nursery worker? She volunteered. Need tables put up for a church dinner? Gladly. Need a luncheon organized? She was on top of it. Did someone need help moving? She'd pack boxes and help load the truck. Every one knew they could rely on "Kay." She'd say yes, whatever the request, and do the job cheerfully.

But Kay was newly married and began burning out. Her husband also had the gift of service, which meant they were both always running, always doing for others. Irritation was beginning to show in her attitude toward her tasks and sometimes toward others.

We took Kay aside, explaining the idea that just because she had the gift of helps didn't mean she had to fulfill every need she saw. She could say no. It was a revelation to her. Slowly she began to turn down some opportunities to serve. She and her husband spent some time relaxing together. They liked it. They enjoyed an evening at home watching TV with no work to be done.

Unfortunately, in the way we humans have of swinging from one extreme to the other (remember our trapeze artist?), Kay began to say no to every request. She spent every night home watching TV. She turned from go-fer into spectator. She needed to find some balance. Kay needed to learn how to hear the voice of God and to do what he called her to do, no less, no more.

One reason we end up helping everyone else get their tasks done, but never get around to accomplishing the task God created us for, is because often he sounds less urgent than our friends. They're desperate. This has to be done now, and they can't find anyone else to do it. Their pleas are loud, and God only whispers. We live the old adage, "The squeaky wheel gets the grease." Our friends' needs get met, and God's call gets ignored. Not intentionally ignored. We just never hear it above the roar of those needing us to be the go-fer so they can fulfill their dreams.

Consider Bathsheba, David's partner in adultery. In reality, maybe she was more of a "come hither" kind of woman than a "go-fer," at least where David was concerned. But we see examples in her life of her doing for others simply because they asked.

The Scriptures give us no indication of her response to David's proposition. Did she say no at first? Did she meekly submit? Did she come enthusiastically? We don't know. But we do know at some point she acquiesced. He was the king; he was powerful. But she could have resisted, even if it cost her life. She didn't. She did what he asked.

Years later, toward the end of David's life, Nathan the prophet approaches Bathsheba with a request. Nathan, who was bold enough to confront David over his sin with Bathsheba, now uses her as a messenger to get what he wants from David.

Adonijah has made himself king even though David had promised the kingship to Bathsheba's son Solomon. Nathan comes to Bathsheba and gives her a job to do. "Go in to King David and say to him, 'My lord the king, did you not swear to me your servant: "Surely Solomon your son shall be king after me, and he will sit on my throne"? Why then has Adonijah become king?' While you are still there talking to the king, I will come in and confirm what you have said" (1 Kings 1:13–14).

Nathan gives her the game plan, and Bathsheba acts as go-fer. We get no indication she questioned his right to tell her what to do, no indication she asked why he didn't just do it himself. She goes into David and makes the request Nathan asked of her. She allows Nathan to manipulate her, and his goal is achieved. Solomon is declared king.

If your thought is, "Well, of course, she'd take on that job; it benefited her and her son," keep reading. In the very next chapter, the now disgraced Adonijah comes to her with a request. Here is the man who tried to usurp her son's place as king. Now he's asking her to obtain a wife for him, to be his go-fer.

"Now I have one request to make of you. Do not refuse me."

"You may make it," she said.

So he continued, "Please ask King Solomon—he will not refuse you—to give me Abishag the Shunammite as my wife."

"Very well," Bathsheba replied, "I will speak to the king for you."

When Bathsheba went to King Solomon to speak to him for Adonijah, the king stood up to meet her, bowed down to her and sat down on his throne. He had a throne brought for the king's mother, and she sat down at his right hand.

"I have one small request to make of you," she said. "Do not refuse me."

The king replied, "Make it, my mother; I will not refuse you."

So she said, "Let Abishag the Shunammite be given in marriage to your brother Adonijah" (1 Kings 2:16–21).

This time Solomon refuses her request, and Adonijah and a few of his supporters end up dead because of it. But why would Bathsheba have taken on the job in the first place? She was a go-fer. She didn't want anyone to be unhappy with her, and so she lived her life doing what everyone asked of her.

The go-fer is liked as long as she continues to serve others. But her value is lost if she steps out of the role and contemplates becoming a performer in her own right. The people who seemed so supportive when she was serving them now have no interest in her. Is conditional "love" worth giving up the dream God has called her to?

The Dung Sweeper

The dung sweeper—or pooper-scooper—spends his days walking around with a broom and a shovel. His role in the circus is to be as invisible as possible while he cleans up the messes other performers create. When the lumbering elephants leave behind a deposit, his job is to hustle in and whisk it away before the steaming mess draws the spectators' attention away from the performers and onto the "flaw."

The dung sweepers of life are also busy sweeping up the pieces, trying to get rid of the mess. They feel the need to clean up after everyone else, to be sure everything looks good for the crowd. They don't want anyone to think a flaw mars their family or any problems plague their church.

When I was a kid we had a 15-minute drive to church. Sometimes, with three teenagers in the car, we spent those 15 minutes fighting among ourselves or with our parents. As we pulled into the church parking lot, no matter how raucous the atmosphere had been, my mom would turn around and smile and say, "Okay, everyone, put on your happy church face."

The dung sweeper doesn't want anyone to know anything is ever wrong, that people disagree, that the circus doesn't always shimmer with magic. Flaws indicate weakness, and we don't want anyone to know we're weak. We don't want our dirty laundry aired in public. And the dung sweeper tries to keep all of that dirtiness under wraps.

They're fixers, making sure others don't have to live with the consequences of their own bad choices. Part of this is because the dung sweeper loves the erring person and wants to keep them from pain. But often the larger part is because the dung sweeper wants to protect himself from embarrassment. "If people knew my kid made this mistake," thinks the dung sweeper, "they'll think I'm a bad parent, that I can't manage my own family." His reputation is at stake, and he fixes the problem so it doesn't reflect badly on him.

We dung sweepers of life usually do more, though, than clean up the mess. We take responsibility for the mess. It becomes our own. We even apologize for things that aren't our fault. Studies have shown women apologize more often than men. It's not because men won't apologize but because women feel there are more things they need to apologize for. Their threshold of what requires an apology is lower than it is for men. "Women, more often than men, tend to apologize out of a desire to seem likeable," one contributor believes.[8]

As good dung sweepers we're busy apologizing for our teen's disinterest, our boss's rudeness, our church's lack of a breastfeeding room, and plenty of other situations totally out of our control. We apologize because we feel guilty we can't present the perfect circus experience to this person. That pile of dung sits there mucking it up. And we internalize it to mean people are judging us for our incompetence.

Another of David's wives shows us a biblical example of the dung sweeper. Before Abigail was married to David she was married to a man whose name, Nabal, literally meant "fool." Apparently it fit him well. Before David was king, he was a fugitive and leader of a band of misfits out in the desert. First Samuel 25:3 tells us Abigail was "an intelligent and beautiful woman, but her husband ... was surly and mean in his dealings."

David and his men had offered protection to Nabal's shepherds when they were out in David's territory. So when David hears Nabal has begun to shear his sheep, which engendered a party, he sent some of his men to Nabal for a helping of party food. Nabal was disinclined to acquiesce to David's request, even when reminded of the care David had taken of his men. David's men return empty handed, and David is furious with Nabal. He arms his men and heads off to slaughter Nabal and his workers.

Meanwhile, back at the ranch, Nabal's men have gone to Abigail to apprise her of the situation. The dung sweeper kicks into action. She has her servants prepare bountiful food for David and his men. She sets off to deliver it without ever telling Nabal.

The Scripture passage goes on to describe Abigail's perfect dung sweeper actions:

> When Abigail saw David, she quickly got off her donkey and
> bowed down before David with her face to the ground. She fell
> at his feet and said: "My lord, let the blame be on me alone.
> Please let your servant speak to you; hear what your servant has
> to say. May my lord pay no attention to that wicked man Nabal.

He is just like his name—his name is Fool, and folly goes with him. But as for me, your servant, I did not see the men my master sent.

"... And let this gift, which your servant has brought to my master, be given to the men who follow you. Please forgive your servant's offense" (1 Samuel 25:23–28).

Abigail grovels. She takes all the blame ("let the blame be on me alone," "I did not see the men my master sent," "please forgive your servant's offense"). She's brought gifts aplenty to make up for her husband's bad behavior. While she does affirm her husband is "wicked" and "a fool," she still takes the responsibility for the problem and sweeps up the manure her husband has shoveled into David's life.

Taking responsibility for cleaning up the messes of others can have unwelcome consequences. The dung sweeper lives with more and more guilt as she takes ownership of, and apologizes for, the mistakes of others, or even things beyond human control, like the weather. ("I'm so sorry it rained on your wedding day. What can I do to make things better?")

The consequences for those she bails out can be significant as well. They never learn to take responsibility for their own actions because no ramifications make them reconsider. And so they often become more and more like a spoiled child (which they might be), going on their merry way, unconcerned about the feelings or needs of others, because the dung sweeper will clean up any mess they leave behind.

Questions for Contemplation or Discussion

1. How do you see yourself taking on the persona of one of these nonperformers?

2. Why do you think it's so easy for you to fall into that behavior?

3. What benefits does that choice bring to your life?

4. What negative impact does being a nonperformer have on your life?

5. Do you think other people influence your choice of a certain behavior?

6. Does being a Christian make you feel you should choose one of these personas?

7. What guilt do you find in your life based on the act(s) you are (or are not) part of?

Chapter 4:
Why Are You Doing It?

What drives us to choose these circus positions we've just talked about? I believe we're trying to fulfill God-given needs, needs God created in us for his glory. These needs are planted within us by God so we'll pursue a relationship with him and live out his meaning for our lives as part of his community.

Unfortunately, we often seek to have these needs met in ways that don't align with God's purposes and good plans for us. We've heard or even spoken the promise of Jeremiah 29:11—"'For I know the plans I have for you,' declares the LORD, 'plans to prosper you and not to harm you, plans to give you hope and a future.'"—to encourage ourselves or others.

But we rarely read on to see how God plans to bring that good future to fruition: "Then you will call upon me and come and pray to me, and I will listen to you. You will seek me and find me when you seek me with all your heart" (Jeremiah 29:12–13). Seeking God with all my heart involves *him* meeting my needs, not *my* meeting them through my own efforts.

So what are these universal God-given needs?

1. Need for love
When we think of the circus performers we've already discussed, several seem to operate out of a deep need for love—the clown looking to make people laugh, the diva craving their applause, the go-

fer wanting everyone to think well of her, and the dung sweeper trying to solve all problems.

God created each of us with a need for love. We often translate this into a need for approval. We believe if someone approves of us, our choices, our behavior, our Christian life, then they love us. As children we perform for the approval of others. Encouraged by our parents, we sing the little song at the family gathering and bask in the applause that follows. We crave more of it and learn how to act so as to earn that "Good boy," or "Nice job," or "I'm so proud of you," from our parents. Children who never receive those affirmations desperately try to earn it using whatever method comes to mind.

But that need for approval isn't something we ever outgrow. I work for myself from home, and some days I get more done than on others. One day my husband Les came home and asked me how my day was. I launched into a litany of the work I'd accomplished that day. Les stopped me. "You don't have to perform to gain my approval," he said. I had come across like an eager dog who had just fetched a stick and wanted my master to pat me on the head and say, "Atta girl!"

God alone provides unconditional love and approval. This need can be satisfied only in him. People will always disappoint us. I'm not being cynical here. We all know we're not perfect. We don't always appreciate the work others do. We have bad days when we're cranky and the ditty you sang that pleased us yesterday now irritates us. We're selfish. And let's face it, some people are just easier to love and approve of than others.

Looking to humans to meet our deepest need for love is an exercise in futility. This doesn't minimize our need for love, but it does tell us where to find it.

In Matthew 22:36–40 someone asks Jesus a question:

"Teacher, which is the greatest commandment in the Law?"
Jesus replied: "'Love the Lord your God with all your heart and with all your soul and with all your mind.' This is the first and greatest commandment. And the second is like it: 'Love your neighbor as yourself.' All the Law and the Prophets hang on these two commandments."

We're told to love God with all we have. And secure in that love, we're then to love others. First John 4:7 tells us love comes to us first before we can love: "Dear friends, let us love one another, for love comes from God. Everyone who loves has been born of God and knows God." If we're going to be able to love others it'll be because God's love has touched our lives, invaded our lives. John goes on in verse 19 to say, "We love because he first loved us."

Without God's love we can't hope to love ourselves or others well. If we look to people to fulfill our need for love, we'll never be satisfied, and we'll never have enough to spare for others. Only God provides unconditional love.

We have a well-known Bible story we call "The Prodigal Son." In it, the father, who represents God, runs for the son who has returned after wasting his inheritance and his life. The father loves and forgives. His love is unconditional. I love the Phillips, Craig & Dean song entitled, "When God Ran," with its line, "It was the only time I ever saw Him run." God loves us enough to run to us, to enfold us in his arms.

But it's always bothered me that we call this story "The Prodigal Son," because two sons inhabit this story. While the sins of the prodigal are blatant, the "good son" has his own sins, those of attitude—jealousy, bitterness, anger, judgmentalism. I think we often don't want to look at the second son because his sins are ours. These attitudinal sins are easier to hide, but they're still sin. And yet, the father does the same for the son with the poor attitudes—he comes seeking.

We have trouble loving like that, even with our own children. And we experience the same from the other side. Sometimes people have difficulty loving us, often through no fault of our own. And so people will disappoint us, loving us conditionally. We're never able to get enough love from individuals.

When you take the part of the clown, diva, go-fer, or the dung sweeper, is love what you're looking for?

2. Need for significance

It's obvious to us that the ringmasters and jugglers of life's circus often operate out of a need for significance. But, in truth, we all want to feel valued and important, believing our lives matter.

In his classic book, *The Search for Significance*, Robert S. Magee says this about how we run our lives to fulfill this need:

> From life's outset, we find ourselves on the prowl, searching to satisfy some inner unexplained yearning. Our hunger causes us to search for people who will love us. Our desire for acceptance pressures us to perform for the praise of others. We strive for success, driving our minds and bodies harder and further, hoping that because of sweat and sacrifice, others will appreciate us more.
>
> But the man or woman who lives only for the love and attention of others is never satisfied—at least, not for long. ...
>
> In the Scriptures, God supplies the essentials for discovering our significance and worth. The first two chapters of Genesis recount man's creation, revealing man's intended purpose (to honor God) and man's value (that he is a special creation of God). John 10:10 also reminds us of how much God treasures His creation, in that Christ came so that man might experience abundant life. However, as Christians, we need to realize that this abundant life is lived in a real world filled with pain, rejection, and failure. ...
>
> As Christians, our fulfillment in this life depends not on our skills to avoid life's problems, but on our ability to apply God's specific solutions to those problems. An accurate understanding of God's truth is the first step toward discovering our significance and worth.[9]

Ask almost any person, Christian or non-Christian, "How are you?" and the standard answer these days is "Really busy." It's almost an automated response, as though being busy shows how valuable and important we are and how significant our lives are.

I spent years working in the advertising department of a large corporation, and I can remember my boss telling me to always answer the question, "Is your team busy?" with "Yes, very," no matter how busy (or not) we actually were. Her fear was if they didn't perceive us as always busy, they might think our team wasn't valuable, wasn't necessary, and they'd cut staff.

As individuals, our "Really busy" serves that same purpose. It's a fear-fueled response designed to ensure others don't think we're unimportant. I'm not saying we're not busy, just that it's become a badge of honor, a way of saying, "Look at me; my life is valuable; I matter."

Who would you be if you weren't what you do?

Ask yourself a question: Who would you be if you weren't what you do? I know it sounds like a funny question, but when people ask us about ourselves, we tell them what we do. I say, "I'm a writer and a speaker and a pastor's wife." I might tell them I teach junior church or I help in one ministry or another. You might say you're a wife or a mother or a doctor or an artist or a lawyer. All of those are important, but all of them could change in a moment. And yet we would still have amazing worth. Those activities, those roles, are not us.

Our true worth comes from a relationship with God, in his declaration of us as worthy of his love, not from any human relationship or affirmation.

When my mom used to introduce her adult children to people, she'd often say things like, "This is my son who is a minister," or "This is my daughter who was a buyer for Macy's." A "who" always defined us and gave us added worth. On the other hand, I can remember my dad introducing me by proudly saying, "This is *my* daughter." What gave me worth was simply my relationship to him, not what I did.

God says we have worth because we're related to him, not because of what we've done. He's placed us in his family through adoption by our acceptance of what Jesus Christ did on the cross:

> For he chose us in him before the creation of the world to be holy and blameless in his sight. In love, he predestined us to be adopted as his sons through Jesus Christ, in accordance with his pleasure and will—to the praise of his glorious grace,

which he has freely given us in the One he loves (Ephesians 1:4–6).

I can hear God saying, "This is *my* daughter," with all the pride of a father.

In addition to being God's beloved child, Ephesians 2:10 tells us, "For we are God's workmanship, created in Christ Jesus to do good works, which God prepared in advance for us to do." You are the amazing handiwork of God, created for an essential purpose in his kingdom. When we recognize our purpose, doing what he designed us for in his Spirit's power, we know our lives matter. We don't have to manufacture busyness because we're living out the Creator's purpose for our lives.

3. Need for adventure

The thirst for adventure is obvious in the free-flying leaps of the trapeze artist and daring actions of the lion tamer, placing his head between the jaws of death. Most of us like new possessions, new experiences, and the adrenaline rush that comes from an adventure. It's why extreme sports have become so popular. And it's the hunger that fuels most advertising. Rarely does the car ad show you a man driving to the grocery store or his office. It shows him on the open road, roaring around S-turns on a majestic mountain.

We often tamp down the adventure need in us because of financial concerns, or our responsibilities, or the belief we need to be a grownup. After all, we can't just pick up and run off after the circus. We have a mortgage to pay and kids to raise. Our lives become sedate, predictable. And, let's face it, a little boring.

Maybe we think that's what a good Christian life looks like. Safe.

But I believe God created us for adventure. He has an adventure bigger than we can imagine ready for us as part of his grand adventure. The Scriptures tell us we can't even dream up what God has in store for us—"However, as it is written: 'No eye has seen, no ear has heard, no mind has conceived what God has prepared for those who love him'" (1 Corinthians 2:9).

I think the Christian life would be much more attractive to unbelievers if we lived it as a grand adventure, daring new things for God, instead of as a predictable routine responsibility. They already know the spirit-numbing effect of a life wrapped up in managing risk and ensuring financial security.

But to pursue adventure, we do need to let go—of stuff, of our plans, of stability. Are you willing? Am I?

I love this quote from Mary Schmich, a columnist for the *Chicago Tribune*: "Do one thing every day that scares you."

My friend Carla came to me terrified a few years ago because she'd been asked to speak somewhere, solely because her husband was in a position of leadership. But she stepped out, prepared like crazy

I think the Christian life would be much more attractive to unbelievers if we lived it as a grand adventure, daring new things for God.

and did it. That first "doing of something that scared her" has led to opportunities to speak around the world. But without the first scary step, she'd never have spoken overseas.

How would your life change if you sought to live adventurously with God? Are you willing to pray and ask God to show you what he wants you to attempt for him?

4. Need for community

Every circus performer exhibits a need for community. The circus provides them with a ready-made family, with others to share their joys and sorrows. It operates in an interdependent way that allows them to feel a part of something bigger than themselves.

We, too, crave community. We were crafted for fellowship with God and with each other; community was part of God's design for humans. We seem to intrinsically know the power of community. "A sorrow shared is but half a trouble, but a joy that's shared is a joy made double" is a proverb in many forms in various countries, probably because it expresses a universal truth.

Sometimes, just to be near others, to relate, we take any job in the circus so we can feel close to someone. Did you ever join a group or volunteer for a committee not because you were vitally interested in its mission but because it seemed as though they had fun together? Or maybe it was because you wanted to hang around one or more of the people in it, hoping they'd become your friends.

This need for community is why Hebrews 10:25 tells us, "Let us not give up meeting together, as some are in the habit of doing, but let us encourage one another—and all the more as you see the Day approaching." God knows we need the encouragement and wisdom of others to live a healthy life. He knows how difficult it is to stay committed to a life of following God without the tangible company of others.

Dwight L. Moody was an evangelist who began what later came to be called The Moody Church and Moody Bible Institute in the years following the Civil War. The story is told that one day he went to visit a well-to-do man from his congregation who hadn't been to church in some time. As they sat before the fire in the man's parlor, the man explained he didn't need other people around to worship God. He was fine on his own.

Moody stood and walked to the fireplace. He took the tongs and extracted a red-hot coal from the fire and placed it on the bricks by itself. He stood and watched it cool from red to orange to gray as the fire within it died out. He never spoke a word. But the man got the point. He was in church the next Sunday.

We need others in our lives to follow God fervently. They encourage us in the difficult times, cheer for us in the good times, teach us in the confusing times, and admonish us in the straying times. Without them, our fervor begins to cool, just like the coal. God created us for community.

This need, though, shouldn't incite us to take on just any job in the church, just so we can be a part of this circus. And we need to be sure we aren't getting new people involved in the church by plugging them into any open slot of service. A shared ministry experience working with others can be a great way to get new people connected to the church as they work with others. But we need to ensure they (and we) are in the right jobs and not just doing any job so we can feel community.

If you put someone in the wrong job, a job they're not designed for nor enabled by God for, it means two people are in the wrong job: that person and the person God equipped for that spot. And the square peg in the round hole will become discouraged because it doesn't fit. (It might be a "thing that scares them," but it certainly won't be an adventure.)

5. Need for rest

The spectator is our obvious circus example of one who operates out of the desire for rest. Rest is a valid need. And it's such an important part of finding balance in the circus of life we're going to devote all of chapter 11 to it.

But the need for rest shouldn't keep us from being an active participant in God's circus. The purpose of rest is to refresh you so you can pick up again and keep moving forward, keep doing the job God has called you to.

Needs Met by God

These five needs—for love, significance, adventure, community, and rest—are all valid needs. They're God-created needs. But getting them met shouldn't be our focus. When we chase the fulfillment of these needs, we grasp but never attain them.

It works much like these thoughts on happiness: "Happiness is like a butterfly: the more you chase it, the more it will elude you, but if you turn your attention to other things, it will come and sit softly on your shoulder ..."

In the case of our needs, the "other things" to which we must turn our attention are God and the way he's designed us. The Scriptures tell us our needs must be met through God. Philippians 4:19 says, "And my God will meet all your needs according to his glorious riches in Christ Jesus."

We most often apply that verse to material needs, and it's true God will meet our material needs. But he'll also meet our emotional and spiritual needs if we follow him and let him guide us in our circus. Are you trusting God to meet your emotional and spiritual needs? He will, and, in fact, he's the only one who can.

It's a reason we should learn to pray for these needs for ourselves and for one another. Jonathan Graf in his book *Praying Like Paul* says, "We need to pray more for spiritual development and less for comfort and ease. We need to pray more for the Holy Spirit to transform and less for things that make the lives of those we love normal."[10]

What if we prayed for God to meet the deep needs of our family and friends for love, significance, adventure, community, and rest by allowing his Spirit to lead them into a fuller, richer life with God? What if we concentrated on praying that for ourselves? What mistakes would we avoid? What circus acts would we step out of?

Breathing the Air of God

A few years ago, I was in a Christian bookstore and a title attracted my attention: *Breathing Freely: Celebrating the Imperfect Life.* I began to skim the prologue, and I felt as though I were reading about my life. Ruth McGinnis writes:

> I thought of all the mornings I'd awakened without a sense of enjoyment for the day at hand; the long desert times when I was waiting for the right circumstances to line up so I could begin to live; ... I thought of the beauty I'd not photographed because I was too busy taking pictures of things that didn't exist, snapshots of perfection, preconceived images of soon-to-be-forgotten achievements. I thought of all my years of frantic questing, trying to become someone other than myself.
>
> The weight of it seemed unbearable—a weight of many layers of protection that I'd accumulated along my life's journey—layers that made my shoulders droop toward my heart and my whole chest feel so heavy it was difficult to breathe. ...
>
> I thought, *All I ever really wanted is to breathe freely in the gift of life.*[11]

Breathing freely is what we want. We don't want to be frantic in the midst of our circus. I believe the problem is most of us are in the wrong act. We're not meant to be any of the circus performers we've talked about so far.

We're meant to be tightrope walkers.

Questions for Contemplation or Discussion

1. What need(s)—love, significance, adventure, community, and rest— do you think you might be trying to meet through your most common circus acts?

2. Why might it be frightening not to pursue these ways to get your needs met?

3. Read Philippians 4:19. How do you think God can meet your deepest emotional and spiritual needs?

4. Does God ever use other people or our abilities to meet our needs? If so, how is that different from our seeking to have our needs met by others or through our things?

5. Do we need to do anything for God to meet our needs?

6. Read Matthew 6:25–34. What principles can you gather from this passage on how to live your life so God meets your deepest needs rather than striving to meet them yourself?

7. How do you think tightrope walking could be a good illustration of the way we're to live our lives?

Part Two:
Finding Your Balance on the Tightrope

What do I mean when I say we should become tightrope walkers? Tightrope walkers, or aerialists as they're more properly known, practice several principles we can emulate to help us live a life of balance. It may never look as effortless as their stroll across the rope looks to us, but it will make life easier to traverse lightly.

What do you know about tightrope walkers? I didn't know much more than they did seemingly impossible tricks while balanced on a thin wire, high in the air. So I did a little research, read a few biographies of famous aerialists. I read about Philippe Petit, the man who once snuck in and walked on a tightrope between the Twin Towers in New York City before they were even completed. His feats have inspired films, including the 2008 documentary *Man on Wire*.

The Flying Wallendas are considered the royalty of circus tightrope walkers, their name synonymous with the activity. Back in 2005 Tino Wallenda published a book entitled *Walking the Straight and Narrow: Lessons in Faith from the High Wire*. The book tells his family story and shares some of the secrets of the wire as well as what he's learned from it that helps him live out his faith.

While the aerialists' walks may look effortless, they're not. Success on the wire requires adherence to several practices ingrained in a walker from his youth. Failure to do so can quite literally mean the difference between life and death.

These same practices applied to our daily lives can help us walk a balanced life, even if we never step foot off the ground.

Chapter 5:
Focus on a Fixed Point

The fundamental key to tightrope walking is to keep your eyes focused on a point at the end of the wire that does not move.

In *Walking the Straight and Narrow*, Wallenda describes it like this:

> Walking the wire is a learned skill, and as with all skills, it has techniques. Here's one we use to stay on the wire. When I walk, I lock my sight onto the end of the wire at the platform out in front of me. I don't allow myself to be distracted by anything that happens on either side of me. I don't look down. When a wirewalker allows his attention to wander, even for a second, his concentration is broken and his life is in jeopardy. Besides, where the eye looks, the body will follow. If you look to the right, the body has a tendency to lean ever so slightly to the right. That's why it's critical to look straight ahead and focus on something that will not move. When you do, you can stay balanced and walk straight without faltering.[12]

We, too, need a singular focus if we're going to live a balanced life. And we need to be committed to keeping our eyes on it, without getting distracted. Otherwise we're going to fall. And it's unlikely we'll arrive at the destination we intended.

We used to travel a lot with our friends Gene and Theresa. Often when my husband Les was driving, he'd point out a hawk in a tree to the left or draw our attention to what a billboard to the right said. He has great peripheral vision.

Every time he did it, though, Theresa would smack him across the upper arm as she exclaimed, "Keep your eyes on the road!" (I've never been sure how belting him helped him focus on the road.) It scared her when Les looked to the side, because neither Theresa nor I could do that without the car drifting in the direction we looked. Most of us don't have Les's ability. We'll drift on the road, and in life, toward the point where our eyes focus.

Even if we know where we're going, a choice not to focus can mean disaster. I go water walking several days a week at our local gym. No, I don't walk *on* water—I'm not that much like Jesus—I walk *in* water. I wear a buoyancy belt and walk right into the deep end, completing laps just like the swimmers (but a lot slower). Sometimes as I walk in my lane, I'm bored with the view. So I find my eyes drifting shut or I stare unseeing at the surface of the water. Even though I'm walking or jogging exactly the same way I did when I was focused on the diving board at the end of the lane, suddenly I find myself banging into the ropes. When I focus on nothing, I go off course and am unlikely to reach my goal.

Solomon gave advice similar to Wallenda's in the book of Proverbs:

> Look straight ahead, and fix your eyes on what lies before
> you. Mark out a straight path for your feet; stay on the safe path.
> Don't get sidetracked; keep your feet from following evil
> (Proverbs 4:25–27, NLT).

A Singular Sensation

Life offers a myriad of objects and opportunities to claim our attention, as well as scores of people who believe it's our responsibility to focus on them. But if we focus on things or people, we won't be able to walk the wire of life satisfactorily. We're going to take a nosedive off the high wire, ultimately disappointing everyone. Did you catch when Wallenda said if the walker doesn't focus on a fixed point "his life is in jeopardy"? How many of us are putting our lives in jeopardy by allowing our focus to jump from person to person or thing to thing?

In our discussion of the juggler I referenced studies that indicated multitasking decreases the quality of our work and increases our stress. Focusing on multiple people or projects is another form of multitasking, and it also decreases the quality of our lives.

Imagine a game show where to win $5000 you must walk from point A to point B in a certain amount of time. The path is clear, no obstacles. Sounds simple, right? Now imagine the entire time you're walking $100 bills are falling from the sky. You're welcome to gather up as many as you wish, but you lose them all (and the $5000) if you don't reach point B before the time runs out. As the bills flutter around you, how many do you grab? Only the ones that land in your face? Only those you can reach if you stretch out your hands on either side? Do you move a few feet to the left and right to grab just a few more? How do you know if you're moving along the path to point B fast enough to reach it before the time runs out? Do you feel your heart racing as you try to plot and choose?

We make our lives frantic that way, trying to grab all the extras we can while still reaching our goals. Most of the extras are good. But there's always more to choose from, always another opportunity to explore or another need to meet or another person to help. Life ends up fractured and frantic. We need to choose one thing—the essential thing, like Mary in our Mary and Martha Bible passage (Luke 10:38–42)—and focus on it.

The Moving Target

We need to maintain a singular focus, but we need to choose that focus carefully. It's important it be a fixed point. If I'm aiming at a moving, changing target, my steps won't be sure; I'll always be a bit off-kilter.

Focusing on a person, or the approval of a person, is one of the easiest—and deadliest—mistakes we make. People change. People, even men, are moody. What pleased them yesterday, and brought their approval into our lives, bringing security and soothing our souls, may not please them today. Worse yet, they may not even notice our efforts.

When we focus on the wrong thing or person, all of which could move, we'll fall. Many of us focus on our families, devoting ourselves to our husbands or kids. It's a real temptation, because we know we're called to love and serve our families. It's a high calling.

But if our families are our focus, if we're trying to meet our need for significance and love through them, we often wind up in the dung-sweeper position. We try to ensure no mess reaches the eyes or ears of others, because that would undermine their opinion of the great job we're doing. It would reduce the pats on the back and admiring glances.

This is particularly true in the church. How often do you put on the "happy church face" my mother admonished us to wear? How quick are you to answer "How are you?" with "Just fine, thank you." even when you're not? When we're seeking significance through our family life, we place the pressure on ourselves, and other family members, to ensure it is—or at least looks—perfect.

Some of us focus on our careers, looking to succeed and find significance in our accomplishments. God does command us to "do [our] work heartily" (Colossians 3:23, NASB), so we should be sure to do a good job. But Colossians goes on to tell us to do so "as for the Lord rather than for men, knowing that from the Lord you will receive the reward ... It is the Lord Christ whom you serve."

Sometimes we like to focus on our jobs because our workplaces give us the opportunity to be known only for ourselves. No one there thinks of me as the pastor's wife or Joy's mom or Eva's daughter. I have my own identity in this place. I'm recognized (hopefully) for what I contribute.

But making our work our focus means our worth becomes dependent on our efforts—and on someone else recognizing them. If I'm working only so a boss will say, "Well done," chances are I'll be disappointed. What if the day of my crowning achievement is the day my boss had a fight with her husband and she never even notices my amazing work? When she doesn't, hurt and anger well up within me.

Getting passed over for a commendation or promotion turns anger into frustration and bitterness.

Maybe your focus in life is much more spiritual. Maybe you build your life on your ministry, either in the church or outside of it. You may see exciting results in the areas where God has gifted you to serve.

God has equipped each of us to serve him and his church. We do find joy in serving in the way we're designed. I love to speak to groups and I can lose myself in writing. I love to teach the children in junior church, and I was thrilled when a mom told me her son who has great difficulty reading asked to spend his birthday money on a Bible so he could read the stories we talked of in church.

The problem with focusing on any of these—families, careers, ministries— is they can change. They're not a "fixed point."

But we don't always find success as we humans define it. My husband and I poured our lives into a church plant for 13 years. God did some amazing things through us and in that congregation. And then it was over. The congregation withered away. Finances dried up. Our only option was to close the doors. What happens to us then? Do the feelings of failure replace the heady balm of significance?

At a one-on-one Bible study with my friend Mandy recently, she pointed out something interesting to me in Paul's great summation of his life in 2 Timothy 4:7. Paul says, "I have fought the good fight, I have finished the race, I have kept the faith."

"Notice," Mandy said, "that Paul says he 'fought the fight,' but not that he won it. He says he 'finished the race,' not that he came in first. Winning isn't the goal. It's finishing what God called us to do. He decides what success is."

When we focus on our ministries themselves, we define success for ourselves. As a pastor's wife, I've gone to plenty of pastoral gatherings. One of the first questions pastors ask each other is, "How big is your church?" Success is so often defined by numbers. And if our focus is on our ministry, we'll do whatever we need to get more bodies into the pew or out to that women's program.

The problem with focusing on any of these—families, careers, ministries—is they can change. They're not a "fixed point."

Children grow up. I find it telling that the second spike in the divorce rate occurs around the 20- to 25-year mark, after kids are grown. Couples who have spent their lives focused on their children wake up and discover they have nothing in common. They're unsure what to talk about now that they don't have to discuss the kids' schedules or problems. They've grown into different people. Life has changed.

Companies downsize. I had a boss once who was a senior vice president for the department store chain where we worked. She was in her late 40s and had been with the company since high school. One day she was called into her boss's office where she was told they were reorganizing the company and no position existed for her in the new organization. Her loyalty, her singular focus, was rewarded with a kick out the door.

New ministry leaders or followers come in and change the dynamics. A friend played on his church worship team with great dedication and skill. Then a new music minister arrived, and they didn't see eye to eye. Eventually our friend was denied the opportunity to serve in the ministry he'd been committed to, and he and his family left the church, disillusioned.

Our families, careers, and ministries may be good, but they can't be the focus. Because it's not just a singular focus we need; it's the right focus, a fixed one, that makes all the difference.

Mr. Right

Hebrews 12:2 tells us what our focus needs to be: "Let us fix our eyes on Jesus, the author and perfecter of our faith, who for the joy set before him endured the cross, scorning its shame, and sat down at the right hand of the throne of God." We must "fix our eyes on Jesus" God tells us through his Word.

Why? Chapter 13 verse 8 gives us the answer: "Jesus Christ is the same yesterday and today and forever." Jesus doesn't change. He can be our fixed point. He'll never grow away from us, never change his mind about loving us, and never decide to move in a different direction that doesn't include us.

So how do we make him our focus in life's circus?

We spend time asking him what he desires for us as we walk this tightrope we call life. He has the plan for us as part of his kingdom plan for humanity. He knows what it takes to make our lives purposeful, but it means aligning our focus with his.

When I focus on God, he gives me priorities aligned with his mission, loving people into relationship with him.

In the Sermon on the Mount, Jesus told his followers what it meant to focus on him and what the benefits would be. "But seek first [God's] kingdom and his righteousness, and all these things will be given to you as well. Therefore do not worry about tomorrow, for tomorrow will worry about itself. Each day has enough trouble of its own" (Matthew 6:33–34).

What does God desire for me to do as part of his kingdom? How can my life be about seeking to live righteously? I need to ask him each day, or actually, before each activity, "What is it you have for me to do? What is important in serving your kingdom today?"

I often have items on my to-do list that are nothing like God's ideas. He's focused on relationships, on drawing people to himself. I'm most often focused on tasks. I've always been that way. In my first retail jobs, my reviews often included a reprimand like: "Carol acts as if customers are an interruption to her work rather than the point of her being here." Tasks are easier than people. When I complete a task, I can cross it off the to-do list.

How do I ever know when a relationship responsibility is complete?

You can't get around the point, though, that Jesus is all about relationships. When I focus on God, he gives me priorities aligned with his mission, loving people into relationship with him.

Focusing on Jesus can also be scary because it means not focusing on myself. I can't live my life simply to get my needs met. This "seek first" passage is preceded by Jesus telling us what we shouldn't worry about. Don't worry about food, drink, or clothing, he says. Life is more than these. And besides, God knows what you need.

I love that after telling us to seek him and his kingdom first, God says he'll give us all we need. The problem is I often think I "need" a lot more than God does. When my grandson asks our daughter Joy for something because he "needs" it, she'll say, "Is it really a need? Or just a want? I want a million dollars. But I don't need it. And God is unlikely to give it to me."

But God in his wisdom will provide what he knows we need. He tells us, therefore, we don't need to worry about tomorrow, because "tomorrow will worry about itself." We need to take this tightrope of life one step at a time, one day at a time.

God isn't some Pollyanna in the sky. He knows life has difficulties. The end of verse 34 says, "Each day has enough trouble of its own." Don't borrow trouble from tomorrow, he tells us, because today has enough of its own. We don't have to pretend life is always fine, responding with "Great, everything's great" when asked how we are.

We can live honestly, focusing on the God who has promised to meet our needs in the midst of the trouble. He's never distracted, never too busy with something or someone else. He's always available to be your fixed point, immovable and all-powerful.

If I'm focused on Jesus and his kingdom, I won't be worried about everything else. I won't be falling off the wire because I'm looking around me at all the other activity in the circus, wondering if I should be over in that ring, if that person doesn't need my assistance, if that act wouldn't be more fun or fulfilling or just different. And I won't be dropping exhausted into the safety net below the wire, with everyone staring down at me, wondering how I got there.

Years ago I had a plaque that read, "God gives the best to those who leave the choice with him." So often I act like the kid clinging to the dollar-store toy that will break in a moment while his parents want to take him elsewhere to buy him a set of Legos. I can't imagine anything better than this that I want right now. But God can. And if he's my focus, he can lead me to that better place, a place where my needs for love, significance, adventure, community, and rest are met in himself.

Questions for Contemplation or Discussion

1. What is the focus of your life?

2. If you were to examine your calendar and your checkbook or credit card statements, what would they indicate is the focus of your life?

3. Which of these would you say you're most focused on—your children, your spouse, your career, your home, or your ministry?

4. How would your relationship with those people/things be different if you lived life more focused on Christ?

5. What are your fears about focusing your life on Jesus rather than other people or things?

Chapter 6:
Learn from a Master

The tightrope can seem like a scary place. What makes it possible for a newbie to risk crossing the wire? Tino Wallenda explained what made the difference for his own children:

> At one time or another I have taken each of my four children ... on my shoulders as I've walked across the wire. In those situations, the children really can't do any balancing. I'm the one who has to balance and support them.
>
> People frequently ask them, "Aren't you scared?"
>
> "No," they say.
>
> The inevitable, next question is, "Why aren't you scared?" They answer, "Because that's my father!" They have confidence in me because I'm their father. They know I've set up the rigging and taken care of every detail personally to make sure they're safe. They know I love them so much that I won't let anything happen to them as we cross the wire.[13]

Confidence in their father allowed the Wallenda children to relax and trust. We, too, have a Father in whom we can have confidence. God will never let us fall. Psalm 37:23–24 promises us, "If the Lord delights in a man's way, he makes his steps firm; though he stumble, he will not fall, for the Lord upholds him with his hand." In the New American Standard Version it says we won't be "hurled headlong." When we choose to walk with God, we won't plummet to the nets.

He's the great Master, and if we follow him, we'll learn to walk well the tightrope of life. We know God has good plans for us as Jeremiah 29:11 reminded us. "'For I know the plans I have for you,' declares the LORD, 'plans to prosper you and not to harm you, plans to give you hope and a future.'" Now God wants to teach us his good plans.

Wallenda's kids had grown up watching their father and other family members walk the tightrope. When they were ready to walk on their own, they had some idea of what was involved. I'd be willing to bet they had spent some of their playtime walking on a string on the floor, imitating Dad.

Scripture tells us to "be imitators of God" (Ephesians 5:1), but sometimes it's hard for us to see what God the Father is actually doing. After all, he's invisible. Thankfully, the advent of Jesus made it easier. My husband calls Jesus "God in a bod." Colossians 2:9 tells us, "For in Christ all the fullness of the Deity lives in bodily form." We see the actions and attitudes of God in the life of Jesus.

The Example of Master Jesus

We can imitate many qualities of Jesus's life—love, compassion, mercy, sacrifice. But for the purpose of our thoughts on balance, I want to focus on three.

First, Jesus knew he was on earth to do the Father's will. This was his purpose: "For I have come down from heaven not to do my will but to do the will of him who sent me," he says to the people (John 6:38). He wasn't following his own agenda, but the Father's. (I know, it's hard to understand since Jesus is God and he also said, "I and the Father are one" in John 10:30. But somehow, God the Father is setting the agenda, not the earth-bound Jesus.)

Second, he fulfilled that purpose even when it was hard and others didn't understand. In Luke 4:42 and 43 we see the people trying to keep Jesus with them so he'd do more miracles, heal more people. Jesus tells them he has to go because he must "preach the kingdom of God to the other cities also, for I was sent for this purpose" (NASB). He followed that purpose all the way to the cross.

Third, Jesus took time away to sit quietly in his Father's presence in prayer. In fact, it was what he was attempting to do—"Jesus left and went to a secluded place" (NASB)—when the crowds described in Luke 4:42 came looking for him to beg him to stay. Several times the Gospels tell us Jesus went up on a mountain or to some other secluded spot to pray (Matthew 14:23, 26:36–44; Mark 1:35, 6:32, 6:46, 14:32–39; Luke 6:12, 9:28). Jesus knew it was hard to hear the voice of God in the roar of the crowd.

Waiting for the Whisper of God

If we're ever going to hear God, to learn from him, we, too, need to sit with him in a quiet place away from the clamor of the world. Wallenda's children needed to sit on his shoulders. We need to sit at Jesus's feet. Psalm 46:10 says, "Be still, and know that I am God." I once heard this verse loosely translated as "Shut up and let God talk." That resonates with me.

So much of my prayer life is about talking to God, telling him what I need and how I feel. This idea of sitting quietly with God, listening, is so hard for me. I'm a bit ADD. I fidget. My mind flies off in a thousand directions. I remember chores I need to do this instant.

How do we get to the place where we can sit and wait quietly for God to speak?

A gift I received a few years ago at a retreat where I spoke has helped me. The women of the church presented me with a prayer shawl they had crocheted as part of their ministry to other women.

When I choose to use it, this prayer shawl becomes my calming blanket, a visible reminder to slow down and be quiet. I place it over my shoulders and kneel by my office chair. Kneeling with my head facing my chair cuts down the distractions for me. I then read over my to-do list, which lies in front of me. After reading it, I place a blank sticky note on top.

See, it used to be if I did pray about my workload, it was to bring my to-do list before God. I would present it to him almost as if he were upper-level management and I was asking him to bring his big rubber stamp that says "Approved" down on it. I wanted him to sign off on my agenda for the day. The problem with that is it still made it *my* agenda.

Instead, nestled under my prayer shawl, I'm struggling to learn to sit before God as an obedient servant, awaiting his orders. I ask him to write my to-do list.

I read through my list first, and then the sticky note becomes my blank canvas for God. I try to focus my thoughts on him and not the tasks I believe await my day. To do that I often sing a praise song

I wanted him to sign off on my agenda for the day. The problem with that is it still made it *my* agenda.

focused on the name of Jesus, or simply whisper his name over and over until I feel my mind stop racing. And then I listen for the whisper of God.

When I do, God often gives me tasks to do that aren't even on my list. You might think that would stress me out, but instead they give my life meaning. I find his instructions incorporate my spiritual gifts. These opportunities would never make my to-do list because they aren't urgent.

Several years ago as I knelt by my chair, I heard God say, "Call Kelly." Now you need to know I hate the telephone. I don't like to call anyone, even my closest friends. If someone calls me, that's fine; I'm happy to talk with her. I just can't stand making calls. I know it's an irrational fear, but it's my irrational fear. My friends know to feel honored if I ever pick up the phone to call them. (E-mail was the best communication method to ever come into my life.) So whenever the idea of calling anyone floats into my head while I sit quietly before God, I know it's a message from him, because I'd never think that on my own.

Back to Kelly, then. Kelly and I were best friends for an intense couple of years while we were church planting in Delaware. We served at church together and got together every week to eat queso at Chili's and talk about our lives. And then she and her husband up and moved to California.

She doesn't like to call people any more than I do, so we talked only once or twice a year. She doesn't even do e-mail regularly, so communication of all kinds was scarce.

The day when I heard, "Call Kelly," was one when I was trying to be obedient to God and his instructions. (Yes, some days I ignore his voice, treating the ideas as "nice suggestions" or a random thought.) I'd also recently heard someone say the first task on your to-do list you should do is the one you dread the most. Then it's done and you don't spend the whole day dreading it.

But Kelly was in California, and I was on the East Coast, so I had to wait a few hours until it was an appropriate time to call her.

When I thought it was late enough to call, I first called her home number. No answer. So I left a message telling her I was thinking about her and wanted her to know. To be sure I obeyed God, I even went the extra mile and called her cell phone. Again I got no answer, so I left another message. Feeling proud of myself, I crossed "Call Kelly" off my to-do list and went on with my day.

A few minutes later, my phone rang. It was Kelly. "I can't believe you called. I'm on my way to the airport to go home and watch my mother die."

We talked and cried and prayed.

What would have happened if I'd ignored God's voice on that day? I believe enough in a gracious God that he wouldn't have left Kelly alone on her drive. He'd have whispered "Call Kelly" to another, more receptive soul. But because I listened and obeyed, I got the privilege of being God's voice of encouragement to Kelly.

And those are the kinds of privileges I receive when I wait, sit with God and then rise up. My day includes some interactions that matter for eternity.

So why don't I do it more often? Why do I still struggle, fight myself to get on my knees, to put on my prayer shawl? Two reasons exist, neither of which I'm happy to admit. But maybe they'll resonate with you, so I'm going to try.

First, while I don't often acknowledge it, I secretly believe I know best what I need to accomplish. I know my to-do list; I wrote it. My day has plenty of practical and necessary tasks I can't simply opt out of—dishes and laundry and grocery shopping and earning a living all beckon. If you have kids living at home you've got meals to cook and car pools to drive and homework to help with. We have ministry responsibilities, too—lessons to write, meetings to attend, Bible studies to read, music to practice.

Because we have so many actual responsibilities, though, we need to sit with God and seek his agenda. Otherwise we get caught up in the muck of the mundane and never soar into the exciting skies of serving the Almighty. My daily responsibilities also take on a higher purpose when God puts them on his to-do list for me. I'm washing the dishes for God. You're encouraging your child at his soccer game because you're on mission for God. That higher purpose empowers us to do the necessary with an expectant heart. God is at work in and through me. And even if others don't appreciate our efforts, God enjoys our obedience.

The second reason I don't consult God is I fear what he'll ask me to do. What if he asks me to do something I hate doing, like making a phone call? What if he asks something of me I just know I can't do? And if I ask him and know what he wants me to do and choose not to do it, then I'm being disobedient. Better not to know; then I can claim ignorance.

It can help to remember God created me. He's the master—not just in the master-slave-obedience sense, where he issues the orders and I must obey because he's the boss. He's also the master in the master craftsman, master artist, skilled mentor sense. He designed me. He knows what I can and can't do. Ephesians 2:10 says he created me for specific work. First Thessalonians 5:24 (NASB) tells me, "Faithful is He who calls you, and He also will bring it to pass." If God calls me, he can empower me to accomplish what he's called me to do.

It's foolish to think I know better than God or to fear what he asks of me. I know it, and yet so often I do it. I fight the idea of sitting and letting him tell me his direction for my day. The funny thing is, sometimes God says things to me like, "Rest today" or "Take a nap" or "Read a fun book" or "Go for a walk in the woods." They're indulgences I may not have believed I could allow myself that day, but God knows what I need. He knows the future, which I don't, and he may know I need the strength today's refreshing time provides to get me through a difficult time tomorrow.

And even when God gives me tasks to do that seem hard to me—like "Call Kelly"—when I obey I receive the joy from being his hands and feet in the life of someone else. "There is joy in serving Jesus," the old hymn goes, "as I journey on my way, joy that fills my heart with praises, every hour and every day ... Joy that throbs within my heart, every moment, every hour, as I draw upon His power

If God calls me, he can empower me to accomplish what he's called me to do.

..." God empowers me to do what he asks of me, and I discover joy and purpose in each day.

We often say we're too busy to spend a great deal of time, or any time, in prayer. When I think this, I try to remember what Martin Luther once said, "I have so much to do that I shall have to spend the first three hours in prayer." He considered prayer his "first work."

When I follow Luther's lead, I find I feel calmer and my tasks seem to get done more smoothly. I have this theory, maybe it's heretical, but I don't think you can disprove it, so here goes.

Sometimes I'll look at the list God has given to me to do on a given day, and it seems overwhelming. It's just too much. After all, it includes many items from my to-do list he knows I need to accomplish, but it also includes those extra "for eternity" appointments.

I've begun to believe, though, that because God is outside of time, he's able to stretch time for me to complete the work he has for me to do. I don't know of any other way to explain how I can so often accomplish the entire list and not feel rushed or pressed down. I think he expands time for me, slows down the clock, if you will. I've no idea how that works and doesn't affect others, but it's the only explanation I can come up with. My God makes a way for me to accomplish what he desires me to do.

Studying the Master

So prayer involves more than me talking at God. It means sitting and listening for his voice. And in addition to speaking to me in the stillness and quiet, within our hearts, God also speaks to us through his Word. If we're going to learn from the master, it means spending time in his Word.

Psalm 119:105 says, "Your word is a lamp to my feet and a light for my path." His Word sheds light on the way we should walk. It tells us of the qualities that filled Jesus's life. It gives us a picture of the heart of God so we know what to emulate.

Unlike our time of quiet listening before God, the words of Scriptures rarely give us specific tasks for our day, and we should be careful of supposing they do.

The story (hopefully apocryphal) is told of a man whose plan for reading the Bible was to open up the Bible anywhere and blindly point his finger at the page, reading whatever verse he happened to hit.

One morning he opened and pointed and his finger landed on Matthew 27:5: "So Judas ... went away and hanged himself." He didn't want to apply that verse to his day, so he tried again. This time his hand landed on Luke 10:37: "Jesus told him, 'Go and do likewise.'" Getting a bit panicky at this new instruction, he tried once more. John 13:27 admonished him, "'What you are about to do, do quickly,' Jesus told him."

The flip, point, read, and obey method is rarely the way to hear the instruction of God.

Scripture immerses us in the mind and heart of God so we begin to understand the broad principles he wants to guide our interactions with others. We learn to live in love, even when it's difficult. We learn to care for those whom the world ignores. We learn to put others before ourselves. We learn to put God first. His Word lights the path that leads to godliness. It's about seeing the person God dreams of me becoming as a reflection of his character.

Scripture reading changes our hearts and renews our minds as Romans 12:2 says, which transforms us. Then as I listen for his quiet voice, I "will be able to test and approve what God's will is—his good, pleasing and perfect will," as the verse goes on to say.

People often ask how I know what I'm hearing in the quiet is God's voice and not simply my own wishes (especially when he tells me something like "take a nap"). When I've been marinating in God's Word over time, I better understand how the heart and mind of God operates. And I'll be able to recognize the still small voice of God because the request aligns with his character. I can be

Scripture immerses us in the mind and heart of God so we begin to understand the broad principles he wants to guide our interactions with others.

assured that the instruction is from him rather than from my own mind; it's his will for me.

Hanging Out with the Master

As we learn from our master Jesus through the Word of God, we need to avoid a performance mentality. It's easy to see my devotional time as one more item I can check off my to-do list. Or like the big brother in the prodigal son story, I might pat myself on the back and think, "Aren't I the good Christian?"

Instead I need to approach my time in God's Word with an expectant spirit, the way I look forward to a lunch conversation with a good friend. It's about focusing on the relationship. I want to get to know who he is, so I'll trust him. It's unusual to have instant rapport and trust in a relationship. We rarely share our deepest secrets the first time we meet someone.

Sometimes it scares me how often I look at my Bible reading time only as a chance to learn some tidbit for my day. For many years I've written a few sentences in the form of a prayer based on what I believe God is telling me in that particular Scripture. For instance, if I read the prodigal son story, I might write, "God I know I often judge others as the older brother did and feel angry my being righteous doesn't seem to pay off. May I look at my own sinful attitudes and give you the opportunity to correct those. Give me your love for others."

It can be a great habit to write down what you learn in Scripture. Sometimes you can see patterns in what impacts you. The danger is, if I didn't glean some new understanding about how my life should work, I can feel the time was wasted. Does that hurt God's heart? Does he sometimes want to just hang out with me?

I've gone to enough writers' conferences that I've made friends with some publishing house editors. I do enjoy learning from them nuances of publishing industry and discovering how the process works. After all writing is a big part of my life. But if all our time together is spent with my picking their brains for information on the industry, are we really friends? No. I'm using them for personal gain.

Do I sometimes use God in the same way? If I approach God only looking for that tidbit to journal about or a formula to live by, am I stifling our deeper relationship? Is it about what I can get rather than about the relationship?

Can I learn to approach God simply for the joy of spending time in his presence, even if I can't articulate a profound truth I learned? I want to get to that place. A few times recently after reading the Word and not discovering some truth, I've journaled something like, "I hung out with God today." I think he smiled.

By spending time with the Master, we'll learn from him, but it will be so much more. The lines between teacher and learner will blur. "I no longer call you slaves, because a master doesn't confide in his slaves. Now you are my friends, since I have told you everything the Father told me," Jesus says in John 15:15 (NLT). We can become friends of God! We'll have a relationship that fills our hearts with joy and in return brings joy to the heart of God.

And we'll find balance to walk the tightrope of life.

Questions for Contemplation or Discussion

1. Is it hard for you to sit still and listen to God? Why or why not?

2. Where do you find it easiest to sit still? What time of day do you find it easier to keep your mind from racing?

3. What might scare you about listening for God to speak?

4. What could you do to enhance your ability to sit still and listen to God's heart?

5. How are you spending time in the Word of God?

6. Do you view your time in God's Word more like an obligation, a search for instructions from your superior, or a time hanging out with a friend?

Chapter 7:
Rely on Those Who've Gone Before

While Jesus is the ultimate master we learn from, we also grow by learning from others who have "mastered" the craft of walking with him. We're meant to live—and learn—in community.

Tino Wallenda learned to walk the tightrope because his grandfather Karl was a tightrope master, and he taught him. Tino's children were all in the family act and learned to walk the tightrope because he provided instruction. He said he can even lead a complete novice across the rope just by having them hold onto his shoulders.

"We learn from those who go before us. They lay our foundation. They make mistakes we don't have to repeat. They give us ideas, and then support us as we build on them," said Wallenda.[14]

God is our first teacher and our fixed point, but he also provides others in our lives whose example we can follow. Paul told people, "Follow my example, as I follow the example of Christ" (1 Corinthians 11:1). Because he was following Christ, others could learn from observing his life and listening to his words. They could pick up an understanding of what it means to live consistently as an ambassador for Christ by paying attention to his actions. So can we.

All our lives we learn from others. As children we learn to speak and walk by observing our parents and siblings. We use the hints they give us to help us learn how to live life: "Put your feet down as you bring the bike to a stop so you don't fall over." "Share your toys with other children, and they'll be more likely to share with you."

We come to understand algebra or iambic pentameter from someone who has already mastered the skill. They explain it and work with us until we grasp what it means and how it works. They cheer us on as we develop our own skills. The same is true of learning an instrument.

Why do we believe it should be any different as adults? Why do we believe in a rugged American individualism that says we must go it alone, achieve it all by the strength of our own merit?

Live as an Apprentice

My husband and I love to visit Colonial Williamsburg. The town was an important part of the actions leading up the American Revolution and in the development of many of our country's original designers and leaders. In the city's restoration, though, in the 1930s, John D. Rockefeller and the others involved didn't just focus on the patriotic history. They constructed a town that re-created everyday life in the late 1700s.

Therefore, craft houses line the streets. When you visit Williamsburg, you'll find the peruke (or wig) maker, the blacksmith, the cabinetmaker, the shoemaker, the silversmith, the tailor, the barrel maker, the gunsmith, the bookbinder, and others busy at work, crafting essential items the way it was done in the Colonial period.

Colonial Williamsburg craftspeople learn their skills in the same way much of the world did 200-plus years ago—through a system of apprenticeship. In those days, an apprentice was legally contracted to work for a particular master for a certain number of years, usually in the four to seven range. His pay was the acquisition of skills that would provide him with a livelihood and, sometimes, room and board.

He'd learn all aspects of the craft from the master. He worked alongside the master and his journeyman (those who had completed the apprenticeship and were now paid). Sometimes masters were legally required to provide a set of tools at the completion of the apprenticeship. By the time the apprentice was finished with his training he'd "learned the ropes." (That phrase is believed to have originated in the nautical realm, but it fits nicely with our tightrope analogy.)

Few fields today have formal apprenticeships, unless you're learning to be an electrician. But most of us still learn our jobs from someone else who has more experience, who knows the ins and outs of the company. If you've ever been brought in to a job for which no training exists and no one knows the job of the person you're replacing, it can be a nightmare. You stumble along, discovering what needs to be done and how to accomplish it, often by first doing it wrong. (It's amazing to me how often people criticize us and say, "That's not the right way to do that," even when they have no understanding of how to do it correctly.)

Get a Coach

When our kids begin sports, coaches teach them the skills of the game. They explain the rules and share tips on how to play better. They help them choose wise habits to improve their game.

We can all use coaches. We're meant to learn from others in the process also called discipleship or mentoring. Mentors or coaches can help us look at our lives and establish our goals. They help us craft a plan for achieving them.

They ask the right—and tough—questions we need to deal with to move forward to complete the good works "God prepared in advance for us to do" (Ephesians 2:10). Questions like:

- What activities or attitudes or people need to be jettisoned because they prevent you from moving forward?
- What are the first steps you need to take to achieve your goals?
- When will you accomplish those?
- What are you afraid of?

Mentors can hold us accountable and keep us from getting off track. They can provide counsel and a listening ear when we get confused or discouraged. They may open doors for us and assist us on our way. They share tips of the trade or suggest good habits to develop.

Sometimes our mentors don't even know they're mentoring us. They may not even still be alive! We may be following their example based on reading their biographies or memoirs, finding in them the inspiration to live our dreams.

We can use mentors in all areas of life: our jobs, our passions, our relationships, our health, our spiritual life. It's unlikely one person can fulfill all these roles. The best job mentor may not even know Jesus. The person who's coaching you in pursuing your dream may know nothing about being healthy. Most of us will have many mentors, some for years and others for a brief time period.

My first writing mentorship was with Jo Kadlecek, whom I met at my first writers conference. I had paid extra to have Jo, a seasoned article writer, critique a piece I'd written. She was encouraging, and we seemed to share a passion for social justice back in the day before it was a staple Christian concern. As our paid critique time ended she gave me an assignment: "Go make a list of articles you want to write on issues that matter to you. Then come back and see me."

I did, and scored another free appointment. She looked over my list, made suggestions on which articles to write first and gave me ideas of which magazines I should submit them to. She explained to me the need to develop credibility and trust with an editor, showing him or her I understand the magazine's audience, before I'd be trusted to write on difficult topics.

Jo told me to submit the article she'd evaluated to a certain magazine she wrote for regularly. She shared with me a trick of the trade that would show the editor I was familiar with her magazine. And most importantly, she told me to use her name when I submitted it.

The advice resulted in my first feature article sale, and it was to a magazine considered one of the best Christian magazines on the market. That sale opened doors to many others.

Jo and I kept in contact for a bit after the conference, but life intervened, as it often does, and we lost contact. I doubt she had any idea I considered her a mentor, but she was one to me. And I'll always be grateful.

Today, professional coaching is big business. The rise of technology has helped because we no longer have to hire a coach who's in proximity to us. We can talk on the phone with FaceTime or over the computer via Skype. In fact, depending on the sensitivity of your job or ministry, a long-distance coach can be safer, because they have no personal connection to the other players.

A professional coach can help you sort through the challenges of a new role at work or in ministry or in life. In high leadership positions often few people living near you know or do the job you are in or aspire to. I've known denominational bishops who have found hiring a coach for their first years essential to succeeding. The coach isn't enmeshed in the workings of the organization nor its politics, so he can help the new leaders think clearly and evaluate processes and functions.

Coaches can help kick-start your success in a new endeavor or help you reach new heights when you've plateaued. They give you a safe place to share goals and ask the right questions to enable you to see your next steps in pursuing those goals. And they provide accountability.

When, for a time, I had a monthly coaching call, I found I accomplished more in the two or three days before the call than in the rest of the month. I knew my coach was going to be asking me what steps I'd taken, and I didn't want to have to say I'd done nothing.

Paying a coach sometimes spurs us on as well. Who wants to waste money paying someone if we aren't going to accomplish anything as a result? When I spend my hard-earned money, I want to feel it "bought" something. I felt the same way when paying for Weight Watchers. I was more careful with my eating because otherwise I'd wasted the money that week.

Be Encouraged by the Group

A group like Weight Watchers or a fitness class can also serve a mentorship role in our lives. If we have health goals or dream of conquering a new challenge, like a marathon, we can learn from others the best ways to move forward. We receive encouragement and applause from the group when we succeed. We push ourselves a bit harder so as not to fall behind or be embarrassed. We know we'll be missed if we don't show up. And they can show us through their own lives what is possible.

The church I attend has a dedicated group of runners. A few years ago, three of the most intrepid decided to do something crazy. They entered a Tough Mudder challenge. As the website describes it, "Tough Mudder events are hardcore 10–12 mile obstacle courses designed by British Special Forces to test your all around strength, stamina, mental grit, and camaraderie." To complete the event, participants run through electrified water, slog through chest-deep mud, carry logs uphill, climb walls, etc.—25 obstacles in all.

The next year 11 of our runners participated. The original three gave them advice on how to train, taught them how to survive the challenge, and provided encouragement and help along the course. It's a group event taken on as a team, and the team members helped each other to conquer the course. The new team members discovered they could try harder, endure more than they thought, and triumph.

Don't Despise the Spur

For some of us, we feel ashamed when we fail or don't try hard enough. To be honest, shame can be a powerful motivator for me. In fact, I left one coaching relationship because, you might say, I missed the shame. I'd hired a qualified coach who happened to be a friend. Because she was a friend, I didn't feel the pressure to please her or, more truthfully, the fear of her disapproval if I didn't accomplish anything. So I wasn't being spurred on to greatness.

The idea of being spurred illustrates what I mean. A spur is used on a horse to get it to move forward. The earliest ones had a point called a prick because it pricks the horse to inspire it to move. A mentor or coach or discipler gets us moving as well by helping us see the pain that results from staying where we are in life. The fear of embarrassment or shame spurs me on to taking steps forward to improve my life or meet my goals.

When the pain of staying where you are becomes too great, you'll change. The pain from the spur's prick motivates the horse, and pain motivates me as well. If it hurts enough, I'll find a way to move to a new place, to change my life.

The apostle Paul uses the spur analogy in Hebrews 10:24–25: "And let us consider how we may spur one another on toward love and good deeds. Let us not give up meeting together, as some are in the habit of doing, but let us encourage one another—and all the more as you see the Day approaching." We need other Christians to spur us on to do good, to encourage us to live for God.

Friends can serve the role of a spur if we allow them to. One day I asked Mandy, the young woman I'm in Bible study with, to pray for me. I had a phone call to make. I'd received a forwarded letter addressed to my mom. It contained a bill for hearing aid batteries. My mom had been dead for three and a half years! I knew I was likely to get agitated as I talked to the customer service people. I

When the pain of staying where you are becomes too great, you'll change.

asked Mandy to pray I wouldn't get angry and be rude when they gave me the runaround on the phone, which I expected them to do.

Mandy agreed to pray. But then she got one of those smiles on her face. And she said, "You seem to end up with way more of these odd issues than most people, Carol. Do you ever wonder … ?"

She paused and got a funny little smirk on her face, and I finished her sentence: "Do I ever wonder if God keeps giving me these situations because he hopes at some point I'll learn to deal with the issues calmly and not get all angry and rude? Oh, yes, that thought has crossed my mind multiple times, and yet, I still seem to struggle."

It hurt a bit to have Mandy point out my tendency to get angry and be rude to the person I'm upset with. But if I'm going to grow into the woman God wants me to be, I need friends like her who will ask the tough questions. Her comment became a spur to help me behave in a more godly fashion during the phone call, and I've remembered it on subsequent "tests."

Because we don't know how it will be received by another, we often hesitate to correct our friends. Therefore, I think one of the healthiest steps we can take is to give our friends permission to do so. We all have blind spots. We can even say something like, "I know if and when you criticize me, I'll probably get defensive, even though what you have to say is valid. Please forgive me in advance and know I promise to give what you say serious consideration and act on it. I want to be a woman [or man] of God, I want to grow, and so I ask you to help me by giving me the correction I need." Mandy and I have discussed this. It isn't easy to take the correction from someone 25 years my junior. But it's vital.

Proverbs 27:17 tells us, "As iron sharpens iron, so one man sharpens another." When iron sharpens iron, sparks fly. Maybe if the verse had been about "one woman sharpening another" it would have begun, "Like an emery board on a fingernail." And while that might not produce sparks, it's abrasive, at least to the nail.

Most likely when someone "sharpens" me by giving me some constructive criticism, I'm going to find it abrasive. And I might respond defensively. None of us likes to be called on the carpet. But if I'm wise, I'll give my friends permission to do so. Proverbs 27:6 says, "Wounds from a friend can be trusted, but an enemy multiplies kisses." Our friends' words may hurt, but they can help. Their counsel, their tough questions make me better, if I choose to listen.

Make Mentorship a Priority

In our spiritual lives we often call coaching discipleship. Jesus stood on the shoreline and said, "Follow me, and I will make you fishers of men" (Matthew 4:19, NASB). A three-year discipleship relationship was born. It was a relationship that involved more than teaching. The disciples walked where Jesus walked, stayed where Jesus stayed. They lived life together.

An effective Christian discipleship relationship allows us to see how the discipler handles daily life. How does she make decisions? How does he treat his family? How does she respond when she's tired or sick or life isn't going her way? How does he decide how and where to use his spiritual gifts?

In the process of living as an example and explaining to us how they allow God to guide their decisions, the discipler challenges us. They ask questions to help us look at our lives differently. They push us to ask ourselves if our way of living or responding is working for us and glorifying God. They offer gracious correction and opportunities for a redo when we pursue our own agenda rather than God's.

I love books and am challenged by reading the works of other believers or biographies of the saints of the church. But it falls short in discipleship because I'm accountable to no one, no one observes my blind spots and helps me deal with them. I need flesh-and-blood coaching in my spiritual life.

I prayed for months, asking God to bring a spiritual mentor into my life. I wanted to be connected to someone who would help me learn to walk the wire in a more balanced fashion and teach me new tricks. In the Christian life, even old dogs can learn new tricks. And I needed someone who would challenge my selfish actions and hold me accountable for becoming more like Christ.

One day I received a surprising e-mail from Margie, a believer I highly respected but barely knew. "Do you do personal coaching? I have really sensed the need to establish some kind of coaching/accountability relationship for myself. ... I've been praying about it for quite some time, and with all the changes we/I have gone through the past year—I believe it would really be beneficial. Having said that ... my thoughts on this are directed to you—is this something you would consider? Would you think about it, pray about it ... and get back to me with your thoughts? Thanks! And even if you don't think this would work with you—I would still love to come and have some fun with you!"

Margie's e-mail shocked me. She's a gracious, godly woman who always seemed to have it all together. I didn't know what I could give her. But I thought about my prayers and wondered if God could be bringing us together to help each other.

My husband became connected with another guy when he went through his formal pastoral coach training. They were required to practice with each other. They discovered their mutual coaching was beneficial to both of them and have kept at it for several years now. I wondered if the same might work for Margie and me.

So I suggested it to her. We had a preliminary meeting over lunch. It lasted three hours. We decided this mutual coaching idea might work for us. We enjoyed each other's company and talked about a wide variety of topics.

Our time together could easily become just two friends having lunch (and sometimes it does). But we work at keeping it intentional. We identify specific goals for the month ahead. We share accomplishments we're celebrating and areas where we struggle. We give advice where we have expertise or ideas the other may not have thought of.

During the month we pray for one another and check up on one another. We look for ways to hold each other accountable. Maybe it's a quick text to find out if an onerous task has been completed yet. An e-mail or card might remind one of us of a verse of Scripture we need. We suggest books to each other.

We're learning from each other. We're discussing the ways of God. We're taking steps we may not have before because we've made the commitment out loud, and we know someone will check up. I respect Margie enough that the shame factor still works a bit!

Who helps you see God's ways, asks the tough questions, and encourages you when you fall off the wire?

Mentors can help us discover areas of life we're passionate about and move forward in them. One day my friend Rita was telling me she wanted to become a retreat speaker. As we discussed it, I remembered an event called CLASS, Christian Leaders, Authors, and Speakers Seminar. "Let's go together. I'll study writing, you can study speaking, and we'll spend four days at a beautiful retreat center overlooking the Chesapeake Bay, away from husbands and children."

We went. The downside for me turned out to be only an hour of the seminar was focused on writing. And the focus was if you were speaking you should be writing so you had books to sell at your events.

The upside was I discovered a new passion. We spent four days in small groups being mentored on speaking. We gave several short speeches, some extemporaneous, others prepared. I loved it and received positive feedback from the coaches and participants. A new dream was born.

I don't think Rita ever pursued speaking opportunities after our training. But she gave me my first gig, speaking at a women's breakfast. My ministry has developed from that event, with mentors who have given advice along the way. They've helped with everything from timing of advertising postcards to contracts to topic development.

We all need people in our lives who encourage us, who help us grow. We need those who will push us to develop our gifts and those who will gently point out what attitudes, habits, or actions are preventing us from being all God desires us to be.

Mentoring can occur one-on-one or in a small group setting. We may need some of each, hearing the input of several people but having one person who can speak directly into our lives because they've come to know us well. Who helps you see God's ways, asks the tough questions, and encourages you when you fall off the wire?

Our mentoring relationships need to be protected. It can be easy to give up meeting with people for accountability when life gets busy. We don't mean to miss. We tell ourselves it'll just be this one time. But one time has a way of leading to two or three, and before we know it, months have passed and it just feels awkward to start up again.

But if we want to grow—professionally, spiritually, relationally—we'll commit ourselves to learning from others. I know when I was in a writers' group and shared goals each week, those few minutes helped me be productive the rest of the week. I know if someone is going to ask me how much time I've spent in Scripture or how I've allowed God to use my spiritual gifts for his kingdom, I'm going to be more faithful in doing so. The same is likely true for you.

So commit yourself to your mentoring relationships. Plan ahead, both for when it will be and how you'll ensure you make the meeting.

Margie and I schedule our next date before we leave the restaurant. How often have you said, "We'll set up our next meeting via e-mail," and then a month or more has gone by without a date on the calendar? We don't want that to happen, so we get it written down right away.

Consider Your Role

No matter where you are in your spiritual life, you can also mentor and encourage others. You may not feel like a "master," but you can be, as the old adage goes, "one blind beggar showing another beggar where to find bread." God wants to use you to help another believer grow in relationship with Christ, even if you don't feel you're always

As you work with people, help them learn to focus on Jesus—not to look to you for approval.

growing as you should. Teach her what you know. Let her follow you along the rope.

You have no idea how your investment of time in the lives of others will impact them. What seems trivial to you may be the catalyst that propels them forward on the tightrope with Christ. Be faithful and allow God to work through you.

I've been astonished on several occasions to receive an e-mail or note from women I've mentored thanking me for a particular thing I said or did that made all the difference in their lives. Most of the time, I don't even remember saying it. I believe God put those words in my mouth and spoke them into the right situation to accomplish his work. Trust him for the results.

As you work with people, help them learn to focus on Jesus—not to look to you for approval. We need to be careful not to insist others do life our way or become part of our ministry. I developed a series on worship for our junior church program, in which we rotate teachers. I wrote the lessons and provided the material. I found myself getting frustrated when people didn't seem concerned about teaching it the way I wrote it. I had to learn to let go. God has given us all different gifts and styles; let each person use her or his own gifts.

Part of our job is to help those we mentor or disciple discover their own good works God prepared for them as Ephesians 2:10 says. If they're only imitating your good works, they won't be walking the path God has for them.

Picture yourself on the wire, reaching forward to grasp the hand of someone who's farther along. She's smiling her encouragement, maybe giving some advice for the next intricate maneuver. Now reach back to take the hand of another, someone taking those first tentative steps in a move you've already mastered. Give her the pointers that have helped you. Tell her she can do it. Beam with pride as she pulls it off.

Yes, to find balance in life, we focus on Jesus and learn from him. But he also provides others to cheer us along and teach us ways to follow him more closely. Take advantage of relationships with others who are further along the journey. God has placed them in your circus for this purpose.

Questions for Contemplation or Discussion

1. Who serves as a mentor for you in your Christian life? Who helps you see God's ways, asks the tough questions and encourages you when you fall off the wire?

2. What are they building into your life? How are you growing?

3. If you have no mentor right now, would you commit to praying for God to bring one into your life?

4. Who are you mentoring?

5. If you're not doing so, why not?

6. What are some of your personal or spiritual strengths you could share with someone else to help them mature in their faith or life?

7. Who comes to mind right now that you could mentor? Are you willing to pray for God to show you whom to mentor and how to connect with that person?

Chapter 8:
Be Intentional

Walking a tightrope isn't something you just stumble into or decide to do some day on a whim. At least, not if you're going to survive. It requires a sense of purpose, knowing what you're going to do and why and planning for it.

A tightrope walker points her toes forward, stands tall, and plants one foot purposefully in front of the other. Each step is taken with precision. A misplaced step means a tumble into the nets, at best, or even death for those walking the wire outdoors where no net is available to break the fall.

When we stumble through life without purpose, we spend a lot of time snagged in the net of lost opportunity. We try to extricate ourselves, often becoming more entangled and wasting precious time we could be using for God's glory.

Paul tells us in Colossians we need to ensure we aren't wasting our lives: "Devote yourselves to prayer, being watchful and thankful. ... Make the most of every opportunity" (Colossians 4:2, 5). How do we make the most of every opportunity?

First, we need to see the opportunities available. So much of life passes us by without us being conscious of it. Our world is filled with so many stimuli. If we tried to process every bit, we'd be paralyzed by our own thought processes.

What helps us function is what's known as our Reticular Activating System (RAS), which operates subconsciously in our brain:

The system's sole purpose is to sort through, filter, and organize the bombardment of information that the human brain is constantly absorbing around itself at rapid pace.

The RAS performs an indexing of the information that enters the brain, and it automatically sorts information from most important, most relevant to you, based on the context and the environment around you. This process is critical, as it allows us to focus on what requires our attention, and allows you to forget about and ignore everything else which is irrelevant.[15]

Did you ever buy a new car and, suddenly, you saw that car everywhere you went? That's your RAS kicking in. The Nissan Altima never crossed my radar until I traded in my Chrysler minivan for one; suddenly it became important to me. My RAS knew that and now brought other Altimas on the road to my attention.

Giving Your Brain Direction

If we want to make the most of every opportunity God gives us to do the "good works, which God prepared in advance for us to do" (Ephesians 2:10), we have to let our RAS know what we're looking for. What opportunities do I believe God wants me to take advantage of? How has he designed me to serve him?

A purpose or mission statement tells your RAS (and the people around you) what you believe is the purpose for which God designed you. It gives it a list of markers to look for, so you don't miss the opportunities to do good. It also lets your RAS know what digressions it can ignore.

Do you have a purpose statement for your life? Do you know what you were designed to do on the wire, or are you content to merely make it across, breathing a sigh of relief when you get to the end of your life? God has more for you! He designed you to be a vital part of his kingdom work, and he wants you to use that design to live intentionally.

In his best selling book *The Purpose Driven Life* author Rick Warren gives us a powerful acrostic that can help us recognize our purpose. The book uses the word "SHAPE" to focus our thoughts.

SHAPE stands for Spiritual gifts, Heart, Abilities, Personality, and Experience.[16] God weaves these attributes together to make you a unique person specially suited for what he's called you to do.

God designed you to be a vital part of his kingdom work, and he wants you to use that design to live intentionally.

Spiritual gifts (the S in our acrostic) are "special God-empowered abilities" given at the moment you become a believer in Jesus. Few of us recognize them at that time, and many have to be developed through study and exercise, but they're already given. The gifts are given not to benefit you, yourself, but "for the common good" (1 Corinthians 12:7), to serve the church of Jesus Christ and the world.

Romans chapter 12, 1 Corinthians 12 and Ephesians 4 list many of the gifts God bestows on members of his church and tell us how to employ them for his glory. The gifts mentioned in these three passages include encouragement, teaching, serving, prophecy, giving, leadership, mercy, wisdom, faith, healing, discernment, miracles, speaking other languages, helps, knowledge, apostleship, pastoring, and evangelism. If you're unsure what your gifts are, spiritual gift inventories available online can help you determine them.

You can't choose which spiritual gifts you want; God gets to pick. First Corinthians 12:11 says, "It is the one and only Spirit who distributes all these gifts. He alone decides which gift each person should have" (NLT). We can develop a gift, but we can't manufacture it. If we attempt it, it's not a spiritual gift since it's humanly desired not spiritually inspired.

Because the gifts are given to make God's body on earth—the church—function well, if we're not using our gifts we're hurting the body. "When we use our gifts together, we all benefit. If others don't use their gifts, you get cheated, and if you don't use your gifts, they get cheated."

What are your spiritual gifts? Do you know? If not, you need to find out, because they were given to help you serve God and fulfill your purpose.

The H in our acrostic stands for ***Heart***. Your heart reveals what you're passionate about—your desires, your dreams, what you love to do and what you care about most. It encompasses the interests that make your face light up and your voice become animated. And it includes the problems and issues of the world that break your heart and make you weep. It's the image you can't get out of your mind.

Sometimes the hustle and bustle and dailiness of life have dulled our passion. We don't remember the last time we got excited about anything. Think back to your childhood and teen years. What did you want to be when you grew up? What activities fascinated you? What were your goals for life before some adult told you it wasn't possible?

Looking back can sometimes remind us of the values and concerns that innately matter to us. Maybe you can't remember having any dreams as a teenager. Ask yourself these two questions:

- What would you do if money were no object?
- What would you do if you knew you couldn't fail?

The answers to those are often helpful in identifying our hearts. When I ask the money-were-no-object question, I often find people speak of doing something creative—painting, music, dance, writing, acting, knitting. That makes sense to me. Our God is a creative God and he created us in his image. We, too, have the creative gene.

Unfortunately, at some point someone told us it wasn't practical to pursue that creative field. We needed to make a living. Our parents were terrified we'd end up living in their basement forever. So off we went to college to study accounting or marketing or elementary education. We may not be able to earn sufficient income to live off our creative pursuits, but we should pursue them just the same. Make time in your life for creativity. The church is losing so much by not encouraging and employing those talents and interests in the church as fully as possible.

An area both questions often reveal is the desire to impact the world by solving some world problem, or at least impacting it for the good.

Think about this: What one world problem would you solve if you had a magic wand that could do so?

We often ask this and the two questions above when we're traveling with a group. It's a way to get to know people at a deeper level. I was surprised to hear my husband answer by saying, "I would run an orphanage to care for kids who have been taken from their families."

I shouldn't have been surprised by it, though, as I look at the way our lives have played out. I doubt we'll ever run an orphanage. (I originally wrote, "We'll never run an orphanage," but I've learned it's foolish to tell God what you will never do!) We have, however, used that desire to care for abandoned kids for God's glory by having more than a dozen teens live with us for long or short periods of time when they needed a stable environment. We allowed God to use that desire to bring a 14-year-old and a 15-year-old into our lives permanently. And even though the older child left after a year and a half before an adoption was finalized, we still believe God was a part of it and we were bringing glory to him through following our heart.

What desires, what dreams, has God placed in your heart?

Abilities—the A in SHAPE—refer to your natural talents. These are also God-given, but you receive them at birth and prior to having accepted Jesus as your Savior.

Your abilities differ from mine (and from everyone else's), and that's by God's design. He wants us to use those gifts for his glory. He doesn't want clones. He wants you, and me.

As a child I took several years of piano lessons and I still can't play. My mother played well and mostly by ear. When I was in college I decided to take piano lessons again to find out if mom was right all those years ago when she told me I just didn't practice enough. As we neared the end of the semester, the professor said to me, "Carol, please don't take piano lessons again. You're wasting your money and my time."

I've no natural ability to play the piano. My fingers are too short to easily play an octave. My lack of coordination means I'm incapable of doing two different actions at the same time, especially playing different sequences with each hand at the same time. I'll never be a pianist.

But I can write. People in the advertising world will actually pay me to do it. I've had articles published in a variety of magazines. It's an ability God has granted to me.

Some of you can cook; some people are naturally gifted with babies. Me? I hyperventilate! I'm not joking here. I've only attempted to work in the church nursery twice in my lifetime. Both times as soon as the door shut, I began to have trouble breathing as my heart raced. And that was with another adult in the room. Each time I fled from the nursery to find my husband and persuade him to go in, since he loves babies. God knew what he was doing when he had us adopt a 14-year-old. Yet you could put me in a room alone with 50 fourth-graders, or even middle schoolers, and I'd revel in it.

If you refuse to acknowledge your abilities, or downplay them, God can't use them.

As you consider your abilities, this is no time for modesty. If someone gives you a gift and you act as if you never received it, that's insulting to the giver. Are you insulting God by pretending you didn't receive a certain gift? If you refuse to acknowledge your abilities, or downplay them, God can't use them.

What are your abilities? Make a list and look at how they are—or aren't—part of your life and used in service to God. As Warren says in his book, "What I'm *able* to do, God *wants* me to do."

The P in SHAPE refers to your ***Personality***. Are you an extrovert or an introvert? Are you detail-oriented or come-what-may? Do you prefer to work behind the scenes or do you love to be the center of attention? God created your personality to work with your gifts, passions, and abilities.

God didn't make a mistake when he made you. Whatever personality you have, it is the exact right personality for you. (On a side note, this also means your spouse's personality is the exact right one for him, and your coworker's personality is right for her, as hard as that may be to believe sometimes!)

"When you are forced to minister in a manner that is 'out of character' for your temperament," says Warren, "it creates tension and discomfort, requires extra effort and energy, and produces less than the best results. This is why mimicking someone else's ministry never works."

So who are you? Take a personality test like the DiSC, the Keirsey Temperament Sorter, the Big Five, or the Color Test to discover more about your personality style. You'll find a variety of tests you can take online, some for free. Or attend a personality seminar with some family or friends and have fun discovering your own and each other's styles in an interactive environment. Knowing more about your personality can help you craft a purpose statement that fits like a glove.

The last letter in SHAPE stands for your ***Experiences***. Even if you were exactly like someone else on the S-H-A-P part of SHAPE, your experiences make you different. No one else has had the exact same experiences you've had.

Your experiences will accumulate as you live your life, and God wants to use them. Your family, school, job, and church experiences are all meant to prepare you to serve God. Those experiences collaborate to make you, you. What unique experiences color how you see the world and function?

Our God is a great recycler. No experience, no matter how painful, is ever wasted by him. A beautiful passage in 2 Corinthians chapter 1 (verses 3 and 4) explains how God does this. "Praise be to the God and Father of our Lord Jesus Christ, the Father of compassion and the God of all comfort, who comforts us in all our troubles, so that we can comfort those in any trouble with the comfort we ourselves have received from God."

Now those verses contain a lot of "comforts." But what it tells us is when we go through difficult times, the hand of God reaches out to us and brings us comfort, so that, in turn, we can reach out and bring comfort into the lives of others. What painful experiences enable you to sympathize with someone else's trauma and to offer them the support they need?

"The very experiences that you have resented or regretted most in life—the ones you've wanted to hide and forget—are the experiences God wants to use to help others. They *are* your ministry!" says Warren.

Our adopted daughter faced a great deal of abandonment for much of the 14 years before she came into our home. And then her older sister, who had also come to live with us, decided to leave. Joy was scarred by these experiences, but they've also given her a heart for others who have experienced or are experiencing abandonment. She's done foster care and shared her story and the feelings of the abandoned child with new foster parents. She, herself, adopted children and she's mothered neglected kids wherever they need someone to step into their lives.

Does she wish she hadn't suffered those traumas as a child? Of course, but she rejoices in the way God has used her experiences to enable her to minister to others. Joel 2:25 expresses the beautiful way God works: "I will make up to you for the years that the swarming locust has eaten" (NASB). God restores those years by using them to impact the lives of others.

As you evaluate all these aspects of your life—Spiritual gifts, Heart, Abilities, Personality, Experiences—rejoice in God's unique design for your life. What is the SHAPE he's bestowed on you? Pray about how God wants to use that SHAPE in the life of his church and to make a difference in your world. Then begin to jot down some ideas of your God-ordained purpose.

You can learn to craft a godly purpose statement through a variety of good books. *The Purpose Driven Life: What on Earth Am I Here For* by Rick Warren, where our SHAPE acrostic comes from, is easy to use. One that has helped me so much personally is *Living on Purpose* by Christine and Tom Sine. It's not an easy book, but it takes a deep look at the philosophies by which most of us are living, often unconsciously, and then helps us craft a God-directed mission or purpose statement so we can live a life with eternal meaning.

Maybe you're not sure what a purpose statement sounds like. I'm not an expert, but let me share mine as an illustration. I have two, not because I have two different purposes, but because my focus has been refined a bit over the years. My first purpose statement was written in November of 1993. I know I used the instructions in a book as a template because some of the wording doesn't all sound like me. But I no longer remember what book it was. It states:

A purpose statement isn't supposed to replace God's guidance, but it can help us stay focused on the guidance God has already given.

> I purpose, through the power of Christ within, to live as Barnabas. I will look to encourage others by offering an attitude of acceptance and forgiveness, by helping them recognize and use their gifts and by rejoicing in their successes. I will look for opportunities to be generous and to rid myself of possessions. I will use my gifts of [writing], teaching, giving, and encouraging in the church. Realizing that growth is a process, taking a lifetime, I will live patiently, allowing God to set my priorities and relax and enjoy the journey.

The word "writing," which I enclosed in brackets above, was a later addition to my purpose statement. I had no idea I'd begin to write for publication until six or seven years later. I added it in so I'd remember to focus on it, even though it could be considered a use of my teaching gift.

The opening words and the last sentence are what, I believe, came from some template. But even as I typed them today I realized how important they are. God's power is the only thing that can help us to live purposefully. I need to rely on him, not my own efforts. My efforts find me caught up in all sorts of meaningless activity, chasing pretty soap bubbles that dissipate as soon as I grab hold of them.

I also need to be reminded, as that last sentence states, that growth is a process. I'll never arrive at living a perfectly purposeful or balanced life. But, by allowing God to set priorities for me, as we talked about in chapter 6, I can relax because I'm living purposefully and life is more enjoyable.

I crafted a second, shorter, purpose statement a dozen years later, based on a verse God gave me for my speaking and writing ministry. The verse is Isaiah 50:4 in the New American Standard Bible, which states:

> The Lord God has given me the tongue of disciples, that I
> may know how to sustain the weary one with a word. He
> awakens me morning by morning, He awakens my ear to listen
> as a disciple.

I want my words, spoken and written, to sustain others, to lift them up, to help them live a life in service to others. And I want my life to be lived daily before God, listening to him, so I could encourage others to do so. Based on that verse and my desires, which I believe were God-given, I crafted this shorter statement:

> I want to "sustain the weary one with a word" so we can
> joyfully serve God in caring for the poor and drawing the lost to
> him.

Just Say No

As you can see, purpose statements don't follow a particular formula. Start by writing down the insights God gives you about your SHAPE, about the special way he's crafted you. Then pray for God to show you his priorities for the direction of your life.

A purpose statement is only the beginning. The next step is the hardest: We must intentionally plan our days around our purpose statement. A purpose statement isn't supposed to replace God's guidance, but it can help us stay focused on the guidance God has already given. As I pray with my blank sheet of paper, awaiting God's guidance, I can ask him how I'm supposed to use my teaching, writing, encouraging, and giving gifts today. I can ask if I should dispossess myself of certain possessions today. I can listen for the names of someone who's weary who needs a sustaining word.

A purpose statement also shows us how to choose the best over the good. We know, if we let them, others will fill our days with activities they deem worthy. You can get sucked into a multitude of activities, all important, but none that use your particular gifts or abilities. You'll end up the go-fer or the dung sweeper, taking care of everyone else's priorities, operating out of guilt (remember the "picture Jesus hanging on the cross" story?) rather than out of giftedness.

One of the greatest blessings of a purpose or mission statement is it gives you the wherewithal to say, "No." When someone asks you to do something not in line with your purpose, you can graciously reply, "I'm sorry, but God has given me a purpose and mission and this particular job (or opportunity or responsibility) doesn't line up with the mission I'm called to pursue." It'll take people a while to get used to it. But we'll model for others how to live out a purpose designed by God.

One of the greatest blessings of a purpose or mission statement is it gives you the wherewithal to say, "No."

Henry Cloud spoke at a Women of Faith event I attended a few years ago. He spoke about "necessary endings." Some activities or relationships need to be pruned from our lives so we can do God's best. Like a rose bush from which a master gardener removes some of the buds so the bush can thrive, you need to let go of some good commitments to pursue God's best. As Elevation Church pastor, Steven Furtick says in his podcast interview with Cloud, "What 'this' will you miss if you hold onto 'that'?"[17] What are the necessary endings you need to bring about?

A purpose statement also shows us how to spend our money and our time. For instance, if part of my purpose is to "rid myself of possessions," I need to ask why I'm spending money to buy more clothes or knickknacks or (gasp) books. What guidelines do I have to put in place so I'm not accumulating stuff? Could I convince myself to use the library more rather than buying every book I want to read?

If part of my purpose is to "draw the lost to Christ," I need to evaluate how much time I'm spending developing relationships with people who don't yet know Jesus. I'm a pastor's wife, which means I'm around church people. It also means I get invited to a lot of home parties, for everything from Tastefully Simple foods to 31 bags. In general, I make it my policy not to go to home parties. I can't afford to buy something at every party (nor do I want to since I'm trying to "rid myself of possessions"). Parties can also eat up a lot of time, and I don't want someone hurt because I didn't come to her party but I went to someone else's.

If, however, a nonchurch friend invites me to a home party, I do my best to attend. I want to develop those relationships. Honestly, I'm no more interested in seeing the product than I'm with my Christian friends, but I'm bowing to a higher purpose. So this week I'll lose a Sunday afternoon to go to a trunk show for clothing I can't afford and don't need because my purpose statement says I'm committed to drawing people to Jesus.

A joint purpose statement can also be important for our marriage and, if you have children at home, for your family. It takes into account the SHAPE of each family member and assumes God brought you together to be used as a unit as well as individually. It doesn't negate your personal purpose statements, but it asks where they overlap and how we can serve God as a team. Les and I both see hospitality as an important ministry God has equipped us both for. And so we work together to host people in our home.

How do the gifts in your family mesh together? And where they don't, how can you use your individual gifts and your family's resources to help each other do what God has equipped you for?

Living on purpose requires prayer and a conscious decision. It won't happen if we just stumble through life without any thought. Make conscious decisions to be intentional each day and keep focused on the goal.

Galatians 6:4–5 in *The Message* describes this process of intentionality beautifully:

Make careful exploration of who you are and the work you have been given, and then sink yourself into that. Don't be impressed with yourself. Don't compare yourself with others. Each of you must take responsibility for doing the creative best you can with your own life.

God made you uniquely to fulfill his purposes. Figure out your SHAPE. Sink yourself into the work God "prepared in advance for you to do." Don't be focused on what others do or what they want you to do. Instead live intentionally and creatively to discover the balance and fulfillment God has for you.

Questions for Contemplation or Discussion

1. What would you do if money were no object?

2. What would you do if you knew you couldn't fail?

3. Reread Galatians 6:4–5 from *The Message*:
   > Make careful exploration of who you are and the work
   > you have been given, and then sink yourself into that.
   > Don't be impressed with yourself. Don't compare
   > yourself with others. Each of you must take
   > responsibility for doing the creative best you can with
   > your own life.

   How would examining who you are and "the work you have
   been given" make a difference in what you do each day?

4. How would this examination help you live intentionally?

5. How might a purpose statement help you find balance?

6. Does your family have a purpose or mission statement? Would
   it help you make family decisions?

7. What is one thing a purpose statement would help you say
   "No" to?

Chapter 9:
Live in the Moment

Living in the moment may sound like a contradiction to being intentional, to living with purpose. But it's not.

A tightrope walk requires complete focus. You need to know exactly where you are and what is happening around you. You need to be fully present, concentrating on this particular walk. Your mind can't wander to what you're going to eat at your celebratory dinner when the walk is over. You can't be thinking about how the last trip across the wire went and what you did wrong or right yesterday. You can't even be wondering how the audience is enjoying the show. Your attention needs to be right in this place, on that tightrope, focused on the next step, and then the one after that.

Part of being intentional is to be in the moment. As Tino Wallenda describes it, "'Being intentional' is to be deliberate, to have full control and understanding of your conduct and presence."[18] I can't be deliberate unless I'm living right here, right now, in this moment, in this place.

Remember what Ruth McGinnis described in *Breathing Freely*—"waiting for the right circumstances to line up so I could begin to live"[19]? So many times that's where I've been, living somewhere else in my mind or my heart.

"Just wait until ..." I say, and I finish the sentence with something like "we have more money" or "we have more time." What usually fills in the blank for you? Just wait until I get married, or just wait until the kids are grown, or just wait until I have a better job, or just wait until I'm thinner. The possibilities are endless. But focusing on what may come in the future means we're missing what God has for us today.

We often have so much on our plates we don't take time to be aware of what's happening all around us. We live by the tyranny of the urgent and fail to pay attention to the important. And because we're so busy doing urgent stuff, God's best may not seem important right now, especially when it involves relationships or those little moments with our kids.

Focusing on what may come in the future means we're missing what God has for us today.

I'm reminded of Harry Chapin's iconic song "Cat's In The Cradle," and the father's realization that if we don't give children the time they're asking for when they want it (and need it), we'll find they have no time for us when they're older.

If you're still in the diaper stage, you may feel like your kids will never be grown. But they will, and you'll look back and wonder where the time went. Let the furniture get dusty and instead play a game with your kids. Create talking time each day and focus on listening. Kids have great attention radar. They know if your mind is elsewhere. Be present when they're talking to you. Listen to the words and to the emotions underneath.

Take some time at dinner to ask each person what the best and worst events in their day were. It helps you to celebrate small victories and to catch concerns before they blow up. Don't minimize anyone's worst thing. Let him feel it and process it.

Friends with teens were talking last week about taking advantage of time in the car. "My kids seem to talk more freely when I'm driving them to and from sports practices," said one. "It helps them, I think," said another, "that we're not looking at them when we drive, so they can share without seeing the reaction on your face." Be present in those times; use them to get to know your kids.

In *Walking the Straight and Narrow*, Tino Wallenda shares this quote from Robert Brault: "Savor the little things in life, for one day you may look back and realize they were the big things."[20]

One Thing at a Time

In addition to paying attention to the important rather than only the urgent, we must stop multitasking. When we're multitasking we're not fully present for any of our activities. Have you ever been busy doing something when your child or husband approached you with a request? You agree quickly and later you begin to wonder what exactly you agreed to let them do. Sometime it can be scary to find out what you said yes to!

Years ago our church had a week of special services. To increase attendance, each church family was assigned a night to "pack a pew." You received differing point values for the people you got to come to church with you: 1 point for a regular church attender, 2 points for a relative who didn't come to our church, and 3 points for a nonrelative visitor. The winners received restaurant gift cards, and I was all over that.

One year my husband and I had two full pews packed and my parents and their friends were seated in my row but not next to me. The little girl in front of them turned and asked me a question while we were singing a hymn. I couldn't hear her so I asked her to repeat her question. When she did, I still didn't hear her, but I didn't want to make a scene, so I nodded my head yes.

My mother and her friend started to laugh hysterically. "What's so funny?" I asked her. In a loud stage whisper, my mom said, "She just asked if you were pregnant, and you said yes. I didn't realize this was the way I'd find out you were expecting." I wasn't, of course, and I learned not to agree to something a child asks without knowing what they were saying!

My husband recognizes when I'm talking to him on the phone and trying to clear e-mail at the same time. I'm disjointed in what I'm saying, or not hearing what he's saying. I can tell when he's doing the same thing. One thing we're both trying to do is turn our office chairs around so our computers are behind us when we're talking on the phone. If I can't see it, it's less likely I'll be distracted by it. But it takes intentionality, the choice to be fully present in our conversation.

The Zacchaeus Principle

Being present for others is something I find illustrated in the life of Jesus, especially in his interactions with Zacchaeus found in Luke 19:1–10. Jesus was more concerned about individuals than a personal agenda or list.

Picture this: Jesus approaches Jericho; the passage says he was "passing through," so he had no plans to stay. People clamor to catch a glimpse of him. Suddenly, Jesus stops. He walks over to a tree. Somewhere close to Jesus is probably a scheduling secretary glancing nervously at his sundial and impatiently tugging at Jesus, trying to get him back on schedule. Jesus is undeterred. He makes eye contact with Zach, perhaps offering a gentle smile. Nothing, not even an agenda, is more important to Jesus than this encounter.

Then Jesus calls Zacchaeus by name. Jesus is no politician wading into the crowd to grab a few hands, kiss a few babies and snag a few votes. He shows he's interested in Zach and invites himself to dinner. Zach knows he's not an interruption of the agenda, but a part of Jesus's life. He's needed by the Master. Zach responds by embracing the message of Jesus and radically changing his life.

The day long ago when I noticed Jesus's interaction with Zach, I named it the Zacchaeus Principle and determined to put it into practice. When I encountered others on my way, I'd stop, make eye contact, address them by name, and show personal interest in them, making them feel valued.

Instead of viewing people as interruptions when I rode the company shuttle that morning, I dispensed with my daily routine of getting caught up on my reading. I looked at each person entering the bus, smiled, and greeted those I knew by name. Encouraged by my smile, a coworker I'd barely spoken to sat with me and we began to talk. In the months following, Kathy and I became good friends. She and her husband Roger began to attend our church. Roger and my husband Les developed not just a friendship but also a mutually supportive ministry relationship.

None of this would have happened if I hadn't determined ahead of time to be present on the shuttle. Kathy and I had already worked in nearby cubicles for months, and we'd never become friends. It happened when I took the time to reach out to her.

How many opportunities do we miss to make friends, or encourage someone, or introduce someone to Jesus because we're so tied up in our own plans we don't even see people?

So many people go unnoticed in the course of our day—the receptionist, the cashier, the coffee girl, the lifeguard, the kid at the bus stop, the garage attendant, the janitor. How would their lives and ours be different if we truly saw them, spoke with them, and validated their worth as human beings, not for how efficiently they can serve us?

One Saturday saw us enjoying lunch with some pastor friends at a small restaurant. The place was pretty empty, so we sat a couple of hours, catching up since we hadn't seen each other in two years. Our waitress, Jess, was personable and funny.

When we live in the moment, we can impact the lives of those who share it with us.

As we neared the end of our stay, our friend Mark asked Jess an interesting question: "Is there anything we can pray about for you?" She looked startled at first, but then plopped down in a chair and wondered out loud where to start. Jess shared some concerns she had for her sister, who was bipolar, and for herself. We said we'd pray and after receiving her permission, we prayed with her.

We continued to talk and joke until it was time for us to leave. Jess seemed to enjoy our presence in her life for those few hours.

The next Sunday, Les and I went to another restaurant. Remembering our experience with Jess, I engaged our new waitress Bethany in a conversation. We talked about the origin of her name and found out she was working to pay for school. We talked about the tasty food. We smiled at her.

As our time drew to a close, Bethany came and thanked us for being so nice to her. "I don't seem to get pleasant customers on Sundays," she told us. Remembering Mark's question to Jess, I asked if we could pray for her about anything. Again, a startled look, followed by a request for her grandmother's health. The restaurant was crowded and Bethany was busy, so we didn't offer to pray with her, but we did assure her we would pray.

When we live in the moment, we can impact the lives of those who share it with us. We can be Jesus in their lives. If my mind is elsewhere—on my to-do list or my dreams or my problems—I won't engage with the present and those in it.

Live This Day

Living in the moment also means recognizing the beauty and moments of wonder and opportunities for joy in this time and place. Soak in the sunset and thank God for it. I'm not a morning person so I rarely see the sunrise. But one early morning driving to Bible study, eyes barely open, I stopped at a stop sign and glanced up to the left. A sliver of sun peeked above the horizon, setting the farm field aglow. I sat for a moment, but a car pulled up behind me and I had to make my turn. I stopped a short distance around the corner to turn back and soak it in again, but in that fraction of a minute, the light had changed. The sun was visible above the horizon and the field was just a field. I'd had only that moment to be present. I'm thankful I didn't miss it.

We often wait for big pleasures, for wonderful experiences, until an undisclosed future date when finances will be better or we have more time. But we're not promised anything beyond this day, and we have no guarantee of improving life circumstances.

In a church we served, we got to know a woman named Ruth. She was in her early 70s and in great health. She loved to travel, and when they were younger, she and her husband had planned grand retirement trips, taking advantage of his excellent retirement package. Six months before retirement, her husband had a massive stroke that badly affected one side of his body. He never left his house again. Ruth traveled alone.

As I understood it, they had never traveled while her husband was well. He was too busy with his powerful corporate leadership position. By waiting for some day, they lost it all.

I don't advocate being careless with your finances or going into debt for a fabulous vacation. But I think it's unwise to defer all pleasure as well. Proverbs 13:12 says, "Hope deferred makes the heart sick, but desire fulfilled is a tree of life" (NASB). Live to find the enjoyment in the now.

Take a trip, albeit a smaller one. Or decide what you're spending money on that doesn't improve your life in the long run and save the cash. I love to eat out, even alone. But when I have the sudden urge to go out for lunch by myself, I ask, "Will I look back tomorrow and care that I got to eat out today? Will it become a fond memory?" Most of the time the answer is no, and I save the money toward something more meaningful to me—a book, a massage, a vacation, or helping out someone who needs it.

Don't spend your time wishing your life away, "waiting for the right circumstances to line up so I could begin to live."[21]

Learn to take one thing at a time and to be fully present when you're doing it. Live right now, not tomorrow. Enjoy this day and the people you meet in it. Listen to them. Then you can see what God is doing around you and join him in his work and enjoy his handiwork.

Questions for Contemplation or Discussion

1. What percentage of your waking hours would you say you spend multitasking?

2. How do you know when someone is doing something else while talking on the phone to you?

3. How often does your family eat a meal together? And when you do, what are the things you are intentional to talk about with them?

4. Where do you need to become more present in the life of your family, friends or coworkers?

5. Are you good or bad at remembering the names of someone you've just been introduced to? How could you focus on being present so you remember more names?

6. How comfortable would you feel purposefully planning to have conversations with wait staff, salespeople and other service providers? What topics could you plan to talk about so they know you see and value them?

7. What hopes and dreams are you putting off until someday? What could you do starting this week to bring them to reality?

Chapter 10:
Expect the Wind

In August of 2011, Freddy Nock, known as "The Master of the Air," set out to break seven tightrope-walking world records in seven days. He planned to walk cable car wires or other wires on seven mountains in Germany, Switzerland, and Austria to break seven different world records.

He completed five of his planned walks and managed to set seven world records in eight days, including the longest and highest wire walk above sea level without a balancing pole, the longest ever wire walk with a constant incline, and the longest and highest uphill and downhill walks.

The two challenges Nock was unable to complete on the days he planned failed because of wind gusts. If wind gusts can stop a man who walks cable car wires in the Alps with no safety gear, it can stop us too.

Wind makes balance difficult. And so you have to be expecting it.

When Philippe Petit was planning his walk across the not-yet-completed World Trade Center buildings, "he found that on windy days, the turbulence on the roof of the towers made it impossible even to stand up without holding on to something; and that the buildings swayed in a strong wind: enough to snap a steel cable tensioned between the towers."[22] Petit's preparation had to account for the wind. He had to know how to accommodate it and stay on the wire.

So do we.

Opposing Forces

Winds capable of knocking us off the wire might come in the form of opposition.

Tino Wallenda, who loves Jesus and has used his tightrope walking for ministry throughout his life, once had a pastor say to him: "God might be able to use you, but if He does, He will take you out of the despicable life of the circus."[23]

At first Wallenda was devastated. But he spent time in prayer. If he didn't have his focus on God, he wouldn't have known his purpose and might have let himself be persuaded to quit the circus. He'd have given up a ministry opportunity that has allowed him to share the need for a relationship with Jesus in arenas and prisons. But he didn't quit, because he was prepared for the wind.

> **No matter how you live your life, you'll be criticized.**

One of the ways aerialists prepare for the wind is guide wires. Wallenda said, "About every thirty feet, we have to attach two opposing ropes that go from the wire to the ground to be held at tight angles so that the wire can be kept taut. ... [These] pair of guide ropes from the wire to the ground [are] in opposition to each other: one to the left and one to the right. They stabilize the wire and keep it from swaying."[24]

In an outdoor walk, Wallenda has people on the ground loop the end of the guide rope around their bodies and use their weight to keep the rope tight. People are pulling on both sides, in opposition, to ensure the wire stays taut so the walker can safely cross the rope.

I like the idea that people pulling in opposition can help hold our tightropes in tension. The criticism we experience, as painful as it is, can perform this function for us. I know it sounds strange, but hear me out.

When a writer has a magazine or newspaper article published on an important but divisive issue, they're guaranteed criticism will come. But the way a writer knows his story is balanced journalism is when he's attacked from all sides.

I wrote an article once for *Moody* magazine, at that time a bastion of traditional evangelical Christianity. The article was entitled, "Does Jesus Want Me to Be Poor?" and talked about materialism and Jesus's call on our lives in relation to money and the needs of the world's poor. It took us months to get this article palatable enough for the audience of *Moody*. It was redirected and rewritten a couple of times and then words were massaged so as not to alienate the magazine's subscribers. As I remember, they still received some negative comments from those who thought my approach was too liberal, too socialistic.

A few years later, *Prism* magazine, which was published by Evangelicals for Social Action, reprinted the article in its e-newsletter. It received several critical e-mails bemoaning my compromising position, my unwillingness to call all people to a life of voluntary poverty to help the poor.

It hurts to be criticized. It stung as I read the responses. But receiving these two opposite reactions confirmed in my mind I'd found the right balance. I hadn't stepped too far from the truth in either direction. I could move forward with confidence I was walking the wire wisely.

No matter how you live your life, you'll be criticized. It's a fact of life. Some people will think you're too religious, others you're too worldly. The same person may even accuse you of exhibiting both extremes, just in different parts of your life!

Ask stay-at-home moms and working moms what the toughest thing to deal with in their choice and they're likely to give you the same answer. It's the criticism from others who think they're doing the wrong thing. It can be shown through subtle statements like, "I would miss my kids too much if I had to leave them for work every day," or blatant questions like, "What do you do at home all day?" Sometimes the criticism comes because people are trying to justify their own choices, and your choice challenges theirs.

We get criticized because people evaluate our lives by their own or, at least, by their own view of the ideal. Like the guide rope helpers for Wallenda who use their own body weight to create tension, our critics use their personal weight—the weight of their opinions and standards and life—to place tension on our rope and move it toward their views.

But if our wire is going to be steady, we need the counterweight. If you're receiving a lot of criticism for a choice you've made you believe is God-directed, find some friends who are on the other extreme to give you feedback from their side of the issue. Don't just look for people who will agree with you, but maybe those who take it further than you ever would so you can find your balance.

We need people who think differently than we do. When we surround ourselves only with people who think like we do, we aren't getting any valid (or invalid, for that matter) feedback. No one challenges our opinions or decisions; they get reinforced. This can lead to error because we're being pulled to one side without even realizing it.

We get criticized because people evaluate our lives by their own or, at least, by their own view of the ideal.

The proliferation of news channels that support a particular political or cultural bias keeps people from hearing any opinions but those that reinforce their own. It leads us to believe every decision we make, every opinion we hold, is the right one. We need to hear from others who disagree. It helps us find the place of balance and helps us evaluate the veracity of our beliefs.

When we see people go off the deep end—the citizens of Hitler's Germany, the Kool-Aid–drinking followers of cult leader Jim Jones, the quit-your-job-and-sell-all-your-belongings believers of a Jesus's-return-date-predicting Christian radio personality—we wonder how they could have been led so far astray. They only listened to one side of an issue, one leader's lies. And the scary thing is it could happen to any of us if we don't seek a variety of opinions and viewpoints.

We need the criticism, and getting it from both sides of an issue can help us know our viewpoint, our decision, is a balanced one.

We don't always need other people to produce tension in our lives. Sometimes our own guilt-laden thoughts will also create tension—Am I doing enough? Am I doing too much? It's the rare person who doesn't question her own decisions, doesn't second-guess herself. And while we can't live in indecision and make progress down the wire, self-examination isn't necessarily a bad thing. It allows us to be honest about the steps we're taking and confirm we're focused on the path Jesus has called us to walk.

When criticism comes—from external sources or your own mind— use it to steady the wire. If criticism is coming from both extremes, quite possibly your life is in balance. If not, it may be time to reevaluate or to broaden your circle of acquaintances.

For instance, if no one at work thinks you're strange for the way you live for Jesus, maybe you've stepped off the tightrope and are wallowing in the world. If you act just like the nonbelievers at work do, behaving and talking no differently, you don't do anything that would warrant their criticism. And yet people are supposed to see something different in the life of a Christian. After Peter and John are arrested and defend themselves, Acts 4:13 tells us, "When [the religious leaders] saw the courage of Peter and John and realized that they were unschooled, ordinary men, they were astonished and they took note that these men *had been with Jesus*" (emphasis mine). People should be able to tell by our values, our words, our love (according to John 13:35), that we "have been with Jesus."

On the other hand, if everyone at work avoids you, maybe you've stepped off the other side and are so holier-than-thou or just plain weird you can't relate to them. If you've become someone who preaches at them constantly or looks at them disapprovingly at every turn, they won't come close. If you take the admonition, to "be ye separate" (2 Corinthians 6:17, KJV) so seriously you refuse to develop any relationships with unbelieving coworkers, you will have no opportunity to tell them of a God who loves them, because it's obvious you don't.

What do your coworkers or the mothers of your children's schoolmates think of you? How can that tension help you evaluate whether you're walking the wire in a way God designed?

Expect Friendly Fire

Criticism comes even in the church, even from our friends, based on how we live for Jesus. When we want to live for Christ alone, we can upset other Christians' cozy normalcy. If we decide God is calling us to do something different, especially sacrificial, our Christian friends can find it threatening to their own lifestyle. They may fear God will ask them to make the same change, and they don't want to, so they don't want us to change either.

For instance, if you believe God is calling you to spend your family's vacation money to go on a mission trip rather than to do Walt Disney World, your friends may fear God will ask the same of them. Or they may see your decision as a criticism of their vacation choice. And if you're trying to persuade others they must walk the way you do, must take that mission trip—you *are* being critical!

The changes God leads us to make can also bring criticism from our Christian friends if it deviates from what constitutes "good Christian behavior" in your church circle. For example, suppose you decide to spend Bible study night bowling with your neighbors so you can introduce them to Jesus instead of attending the study. Other church members might think you're decidedly unspiritual for missing a vital church meeting. And they might be very vocal about it!

Know you are in good company. The Pharisees tried to reign in Jesus for his odd behavior as well. They come to him and say, "John's disciples often fast and pray, and so do the disciples of the Pharisees, but yours go on eating and drinking" (Luke 5:33). What they're communicating are the messages "Everybody religious does it this way" and "You're doing it wrong" (to quote one of our family's favorite lines from the movie *Mr. Mom*).

Jesus hears their criticism but doesn't change. Through some strange analogies about new and old clothes and wineskins he tells them he's going to be different. In a similar incident in Matthew 15, Jesus responds and says the Pharisees honor God with their lips but not their hearts. His disciples get nervous and ask in verse 12, "Do you know that the Pharisees were offended when they heard this?" Jesus did and he didn't back down.

In a speaking seminar I attended, the instructor talked on how she handles criticism after a speech. "I simply smile and respond, 'Thank you, I'll take that under consideration.'" It keeps the other person from arguing because you didn't disagree with them, but you aren't promising to change either. At a later time, when she wasn't tired and emotional, she considered if the criticism contained any truth and, if so, applied it. If not, she let it go. (I want to learn to say "prayerful consideration"; then it's "God's fault" if I don't please my critic!)

We always seem so shocked when people oppose us or criticize us. Why? It's what spectators do best, and spectators always outnumber performers in the circus. Everyone thinks they can tell us what we should have done, because they don't have to actually do it. They don't need to live with the details and the nuances and the surprises life sends our way. They also aren't hearing what the voice of God is saying specifically to you.

Recognize Your Spiritual Enemies

Plan for spiritual opposition. Expect that if you're going to follow the path God has for you, the forces of evil aren't going to approve. Satan will send others to discourage us, to sidetrack us, to guilt us into changing course. And he can even use other Christians quite effectively in the process.

In the book of Nehemiah we read of the people of Israel trying to rebuild the walls of Jerusalem. They have a dream, a vision, and they set out with enthusiasm to act on it. But the others around them aren't happy. They don't want Jerusalem rebuilt. More importantly, they don't want the Jews to be successful.

And so they rise up to oppose them. First it's simple joking insults: "What are those feeble Jews doing?" (Nehemiah 4:2) and "What they are building—if even a fox climbed up on it, he would break down their wall of stones!" (Nehemiah 4:3). People often start their opposition to us by making wisecracks, being snarky. They test the waters, seeing if others will go along with them. If anyone else calls them on the carpet for it, they can reply, "Jeez, I was only kidding around. Can't anyone take a joke?" But if people agree and join them in it, they continue the campaign to discourage.

When the insults don't stop the Jews, the critics step up the torment. "They all plotted together to come and fight against Jerusalem and stir up trouble against it" (Nehemiah 4:8). If we stand strong in the wind, moving along the tightrope God has called us to walk, those who oppose us may look for new ways to "stir up trouble" against us. Like Nehemiah, we'll need to keep turning to God in prayer, asking for his strength to complete the calling he's given to us.

Those opposed to the Jews tried a final tactic: They questioned the motives of the people and, especially, of the leader. "You're going to revolt, and you, Nehemiah, are planning to become king. Wait until King Artaxerxes hears about this!" (Nehemiah 6:5–7, paraphrased). When you live the life God has designed for you, others may question your motives. They may claim you're looking for attention and personal glory or you've "gotten too big for your britches." Take a moment in prayer to examine your motives, and then if you find no truth in what they say, ask God like Nehemiah did to "strengthen my hands" (Nehemiah 6:9) and keep pursuing your goal.

> **When you live the life God has designed for you, others may question your motives.**

We can't live our lives by allowing the criticism of others to keep us from walking the path God has called us to walk. If we're susceptible to playing the clown, wanting others to be happy at all costs to ourselves, we can be tempted to abandon our wire when someone disapproves of our choices so we make them happy. If we're divas, who need the applause of the crowd, criticism can cause us alter our behavior to win their approval.

Instead we need to remember we're tightrope walkers, choosing to focus on Jesus and what he desires of us. We "perform" for an audience of one. We live our lives to please God. We need to respond as the apostles did when threatened by the Jewish leaders: "We must obey God rather than men" (Acts 5:29).

It's most important we seek what God has for us and stick with it even when the winds of opposition blow. Find some friends to help you stay strong in the wind. Ask people to specifically pray you'll fulfill the mission to which God has called you. Give them a copy of your purpose statement and encourage them check in with you to see how you're doing in living it intentionally. When the winds come, call them, text them, or Facebook them and ask for special prayer.

Put on Trial

Trials are another wind that will blow into your life. Matthew 6:34 tells us "not [to] worry about tomorrow ... Each day has enough trouble of its own." Trials arrive in all of our lives, and each day has its own. Cars break down, children rebel, we get sick, our parents become frail, jobs end, marriages dissolve, loved ones die, houses don't sell, friends betray us, our daughter doesn't make the team, our son isn't accepted into his dream college.

Large and small, the trials come. We live in a fallen world that comes with problems. The wind of trial might be a mighty hurricane-like force that sweeps into our lives wreaking a swath of destruction across our lives. Or it might be a steady buffeting from smaller winds that just don't seem to stop until we're bowed over like the tree at the top of a ridge. Those small trials that come one after another are like being pecked to death by a duck. We succumb slowly and painfully to the disintegration of our dreams, finding we've no energy for even the basic needs of life.

How will you handle the trials that enter your life?

Some people turn from God when they experience illness or death. We had a guy I'll call Henry in our church who was a great encouragement to my husband Les. They got together to study the Bible and pray for one another. Henry's wife had a chronic illness. They had been to all sorts of doctors, tried all types of treatment, including experimental ones, and nothing had helped. I'm sure they could identify with the bleeding woman described in Mark 5:26: "She had suffered a great deal under the care of many doctors and had spent all she had, yet instead of getting better she grew worse." Our prayers for her healing produced no visible change.

One day Henry walked into church and told Les, "I'm done with all this. It doesn't work for me." He left the church and went on with his life. God hadn't come through for him. And if God wasn't going to provide what Henry wanted, what he believed his wife needed, he wanted nothing more to do with God.

Other people, when confronted with trials, keep their focus on Christ, on that fixed point at the end of the wire that doesn't change. My brother Bobby will always tell you life is good no matter what's going on in his life, no matter what wind of trial is blowing through. "Romans 8:28 is still in the Bible," he says in a singsong voice. But I know he believes it: "And we know that all things work together for good to them that love God, to them who are the called according to his purpose" (KJV). God will somehow take this awful thing and reshape it, crafting something good in Bobby's life.

"Romans 8:28 is still in the Bible" is our hokey family rallying cry, and yet it strengthens our trust in God. He's present, here with us in our trials. He may not deliver us from them, but he'll stand with us in them.

Many people have found comfort over the years from the "Footprints" poem that tells us God carries us through the most difficult times of our lives. I find more comfort in the cartoon twist posted on Facebook a few months ago. In the first frame, Jesus says, "Where you see one set of footprints is where I carried you." The second frame continues: "And that long groove is where I dragged you kicking and screaming."

Sometimes he does have to drag me along. Life can be hard. But God is good.

Jesus never promises us smooth sailing (and in fact, you can't sail without wind). He seems to promise just the opposite: "In this world you will have trouble," he tells us in John 16:33. Not "you might," but "you will." This is a promise from God I've never seen displayed on a t-shirt No one I know has a bumper sticker displaying it. And though my husband collects refrigerator magnets, we don't have one cheerfully declaring this promise from God. And yet it is a promise. God doesn't want us to be surprised. In a fallen, broken world, we certainly will have difficulties.

The certainty of trouble (translated "tribulation" in some versions) is what makes the rest of the verse such a glorious promise: "I have told you these things, so that in me you may have peace. In this world you will have trouble. But take heart! I have overcome the world." Trouble comes in this life. But Jesus will overcome and bring peace.

Knowing wind will come helps us to prepare. We won't be surprised by the criticism from either side, the spiritual opposition, or the trials. Instead, we can get back to being focused on Jesus, living intentionally in this moment.

Questions for Contemplation or Discussion

1. How well do you handle criticism? Is it worse if it comes from friends, family or strangers?

2. What friends do you have who are brave enough to disagree with you? How do you seek out information and opinions that don't simply reinforce your own?

3. If you are a people pleaser like the clown, how do you stick to what you believe God is asking you to do when others think the action is unwise?

4. Do you expect trouble to come in your life? How do you use that knowledge to prepare for difficult times?

5. What Scripture verses do you turn to when life gets difficult?

Chapter 11:
Know When to Rest

Do you know how much those balancing poles aerialists carry weigh? About 50 pounds. While walking a long tightrope, particularly outside where they've been buffeted by wind, they need to take time to rest.

One of my favorite paragraphs in Wallenda's book concerns this. He talks about a walk taken at the Arizona State Fair:

> The walk was so long [1250 feet, about the length of four football fields] that I had to stop four times to rest, because my arms were going to sleep from the pressure of holding the balancing pole. To get the circulation going and get blood back into my arms, I put my pole down on the wire and stood on my head. It thrilled the crowd, but it had practical application for me.[25]

I'll never look at tightrope walkers' tricks in the same way again. I'll be wondering if they're really taking a rest break. But it proves to me aerialists are smart. They know when to rest, to take a break.

When was the last time you rested?

Sometimes we seem to believe we can't ever relax. If we do, our world will fall apart. After all, maybe you're the one who keeps your house running smoothly. If you took a day or two off, no one would be able to find matching socks and they'd all eat nothing but junk food from a ripped-open cellophane bag.

You can't imagine your church or nonprofit organization surviving if you took a quarter off. Who would teach that class? Who would run the potlucks? Who would take care of all the tasks you handle, albeit grudgingly at times?

Maybe your workplace is the domain you rule. You could be the boss, keeping everyone focused in the right direction. Or you may not be in charge, but you're the cog that holds it all together. My husband's secretary once had a sign that read, "Do you want to talk to the boss or the person who knows what's going on?" Maybe you're the behind-the-scenes gremlin who secretly runs the whole shooting match.

I once worked in the advertising department of a credit card company. I was responsible for ensuring all the correct legal disclaimers were in place on all of the mailings that went out about its newest and hottest product line. I kept track of all the nuances of the product benefits and which offer got what legal copy. When I resigned, my boss panicked. "What are we going to do without you?" she said. "Look, spend these two weeks before you go getting everything you know about the product down in a manual so we know what to do."

I painstakingly wrote her manual. She was so grateful when I assured her I'd be happy to answer their questions if they called or e-mailed me.

They never called. Or e-mailed. Six years later I returned to work in the same department. My former boss was still there. "Hey, guess what I discovered just the other day in my drawer?" she said to me. "That manual you wrote before you left. I'm not sure we ever even used it. How funny is it that I still have it?"

None of us is that necessary.

The world goes on. Maybe not in the way we'd do it, but they figure it out. They handle it. They create their own processes. They do without some event you thought was vital but they don't seem to miss. They find food to feed themselves. They wear their socks mismatched (which is quite in style now, as my favorite sock brand—Little MissMatched—is proof of).

If we're honest, we'll often find our decision never to rest is rooted in our need to feel loved, to be necessary, to find significance, to become part of a community. But God wants to give us our significance. He wants us to know we're loved because we are his, not because of how we perform.

We didn't earn his love for us to begin with. And we don't keep it by doing good works either:

> But when the kindness and love of God our Savior appeared, he saved us, not because of righteous things we had done, but because of his mercy. He saved us through the washing of rebirth and renewal by the Holy Spirit, whom he poured out on us generously through Jesus Christ our Savior, so that, having been justified by his grace, we might become heirs having the hope of eternal life (Titus 3:4–7).

Romans 5:8 says he loved us "while we were still sinners," and 1 John 3:1 tells us he "lavished" love on us.

God's Cycle of Renewal

Part of his lavish love is wanting what is best for us, and he knows we need rest. He created us, so he knows how our bodies work with the greatest efficiency and health. Everything in the created realm has cycles of productivity and rest: The plant kingdom with growing time, harvest time, and then the fallow winter. The animal kingdom with hibernation and daily sleep, whether they're nocturnal or diurnal. Why would we be the exception?

God says we need rest. He himself rested after creation, so who are we to think we don't need it? If the perfect God rested, obviously the need for rest isn't a weakness. It's part of perfection.

Taking a Sabbath rest was encoded in God's Big Ten:

> Remember the Sabbath day by keeping it holy. Six days you shall labor and do all your work, but the seventh day is a Sabbath to the Lord your God. On it you shall not do any work, neither you, nor your son or daughter, nor your manservant or maidservant, nor your animals, nor the alien within your gates. For in six days the Lord made the heavens and the earth, the sea, and all that is in them, but he rested on the seventh day. Therefore the Lord blessed the Sabbath day and made it holy (Exodus 20:8–11).

We seem to take the rest of the Ten Commandments very seriously. We teach our children not to swear or lie or steal and punish them for doing so. We insist they obey their parents. We can't imagine murdering someone or committing adultery, and we harshly judge those who do.

If the perfect God rested, obviously the need for rest isn't a weakness. It's part of perfection.

And yet when it comes to the commandment for a day without work, we're strangely silent. Most of us can't even imagine it. We don't have the "manservant or maidservant" spoken of in the commandment, and so we justify our own need to work every day to keep up with the workload.

Sweet Slumber

But rest isn't just a one-day-a-week necessity. From our local paper yesterday this headline blared: "Poor Sleep Alters Genes, Raises Risk of Disease." The article, based on a study published in the *Proceedings of the National Academy of Sciences*, says, "Just a week of inadequate sleep can alter the activity of hundreds of genes." Inadequate sleep, the National Institutes of Health reports, brings "a higher risk of heart disease, kidney disease, high blood pressure, obesity, diabetes and depression."[26]

Is your lack of sleep making you sick? If only a week of poor sleep can alter our genes, imagine what years of it is doing to our bodies. Experts say we need between seven and nine hours of sleep a night. I know few people who consistently get that.

Years ago my husband, our daughter, and I went on a vacation to Williamsburg, Virginia. It was a stressful time in our lives, and we were all physically and emotionally worn out. We decided everyone would sleep until they awoke naturally. Because the Hampton Inn had free breakfast, whoever awoke first would quietly dress and go downstairs and eat. I woke every day after exactly nine hours and 15 minutes of sleep, no matter what time we went to bed. I've tested it, and I know that amount is my optimal.

When I worked a job in which I needed to leave at seven for the office, getting nine-plus hours of sleep seemed impossible. I was up at 5:30 at the latest. That would have meant being in bed and asleep by 8:15. We weren't even home from church meetings at that time of night!

Now that I work from home, I can sleep later. But I'm still not getting nine-plus hours consistently because I choose to stay up late watching TV or playing on my computer. Many nights I'm not even meeting the lowest edge of that seven- to nine-hour range. How is my health affected?

And yet knowing it isn't healthy not to get proper rest hasn't led to a change in my behavior. Somehow, this is one of those areas we seem to fudge on. We know the truth, but we choose to believe we're the exception. People take pride in how little sleep they can live on.

What changes do you need to make to get more sleep? If for a week or two you slept until you woke up feeling rested, what would your optimal sleep amount be? If you're sleep-deprived it might take some time to find out. You may have your body conditioned to survive on less sleep, and so you might wake after six hours. Or if given the freedom to get its rest, your body might sleep for hours and hours.

When I was in college and trying to survive on late nights and early mornings, my body would occasionally rebel. Once I awoke to discover I'd slept through my alarm, and it was now one p.m. and I'd missed a final. I railed at my roommates for not waking me up since they were in the same class. "Carol, we tried, we really did, but you wouldn't move." I don't remember how I convinced the professor to let me make up the final, but I do remember being frightened my body had insisted on 14 hours of sleep and I hadn't been able to stop it.

The same thing has happened a few other times in my life. My body, needing nine and a quarter hours of sleep, says, "Enough! You've abused me and I won't take it anymore." Now I tend to sleep in a day or two a week, which holds the collapse at bay but isn't that healthy either. Our bodies function best on a rhythm, and short nights interspersed with long ones don't give us that.

Refreshing Our Soul

Rest doesn't always mean sleep. What do you do to refresh and rest your mind during the day? An outdoor walk if the weather is agreeable—breathing fresh air, viewing trees and flowers, hearing the birds—has a powerful renewing ability.

I love to picture Adam and Eve walking with God "in the garden in the cool of the day" (Genesis 3:8). I assume it must have been their custom since after Adam and Eve ate the fruit they hid from God as he came walking.

About a half an hour from my home is a park with a walking/biking trail along a river. It's shaded by trees almost the whole length. Nothing refreshes me more than walking there. I listen to the river tumble over the rocks, hear the birds chat excitedly. I watch the geese peck for food and the fish swim around the rocks. Once I saw a doe and her two fawns walk silently down the path and return to the woods. Another time I made eye contact with a mink as it skulked along the water's edge. Herons fly by or perch on logs to fish in the water.

Nothing refreshes my body, mind, and soul like that park. When I was dealing with a flare-up of my autoimmune disorder and couldn't walk, I'd drive to the park, hobble to the nearest bench and sit and watch the river go by. I'd read or sing hymns of praise to the creator of it all. One day I tuned into my different senses one at a time and recorded what I heard, saw, smelled, and felt.

Maybe you're one of the people who finds refreshment actually playing in the dirt, gardening. For some that's a restful activity. For me it's torture. You must know yourself and do what brings you rest.

Some find playing with their pets or even walking the dog a way to reenergize. For others it might be a game of tag with the kids or a morning spent lounging with the family on your bed and ending with a pillow fight.

A lovely meal in a quiet restaurant refreshes my husband and me. We love savoring the tastes of flavorfully prepared delicacies. Maybe you love wandering the flea market in search of the perfect treasure. And don't forget the massage or spa visit option.

Make time for whatever refreshes, relaxes, and rejuvenates you. Maybe you don't have the money for a gourmet meal out. Can you pick up some fresh seafood and cook at home, adding a few restaurant touches? I realized I love to eat out because my favorite restaurants provide some type of great bread before the meal, served with olive oil and herbs or cinnamon butter or just good soft butter. Bread isn't a staple at our evening meals at home. But if I want to make a home meal a special rejuvenating one for us, a loaf of crusty bread and an olive oil dip will contribute to that.

Rest is part of God's creative plan for us.

Rest is part of God's creative plan for us. He knows we need time to be refreshed, to refill our emotional coffers and allow our minds to slow down. Jesus took time away from the crowds to be alone with his Father. Our resting time can include sitting quietly in God's presence, listening to his heart of love speaking to our hearts.

Out of the Game

When we refuse to rest, we eventually burn out. It may include a physical collapse like my long hours of sleeping without awaking. Or an emotional collapse could mean everything brings you to tears or the opposite, where nothing touches you and you feel like you're observing others from underwater. Your burnout might manifest itself by quitting everything you're involved in or, for some, even quitting their families. Spiritually you could turn away from God and his people because you just can't take the pressure anymore.

In one or many ways we become permanent spectators. We refuse to act. We watch others and, if we haven't lost all energy, we might criticize. Bitterness often sets in because life isn't what we expected. Christianity isn't what we were promised. If we can feel at all, we feel duped.

That's not how it's supposed to work.

Matthew 11:28–30 in *The Message* beautifully communicates God's desire for us:

Are you tired? Worn out? Burned out on religion? Come to me. Get away with me and you'll recover your life. I'll show you how to take a real rest. Walk with me and work with me—watch how I do it. Learn the unforced rhythms of grace. I won't lay anything heavy or ill-fitting on you. Keep company with me and you'll learn to live freely and lightly.

"The unforced rhythms of grace"—do you live in them? Does the rhythm of your day include rest? Would anyone, including you, use "freely and lightly" to describe how you're living your days?

Burnout may also be the result of taking on "ill-fitting" responsibilities God never intended us to have. Our own need to feel important, or our willingness to be guilted into service based on others' priorities, brings a heavy burden that can cost us our rest and, ultimately, our health.

God wants us to learn to rest with him, to take time out. If we pay attention to his rhythm for our lives, it will include rest; rest that will enable us to walk the wire "freely and lightly," displaying God's power and grace.

What steps do you need to take to put your "balancing pole" down on the wire? Spend some time sitting before God and ask him what you need to let go of, or say no to, so you have times of refreshment and rejuvenation. Ask others to hold you accountable for getting enough rest. Consider it a spiritual discipline that will allow you to live in joyous balance.

Questions for Contemplation or Discussion

1. Do you take a Sabbath? What does it look like?

2. What activities refresh your soul and rejuvenate your mind?

3. Reread Matthew 11:28–30 from *The Message*:
   > Are you tired? Worn out? Burned out on religion?
   > Come to me. Get away with me and you'll recover your
   > life. I'll show you how to take a real rest. Walk with me
   > and work with me—watch how I do it. Learn the
   > unforced rhythms of grace. I won't lay anything heavy
   > or ill-fitting on you. Keep company with me and you'll
   > learn to live freely and lightly.

   Would you answer "Yes" to any of those first three questions
   Jesus asks? Which of the things he offers in the sentences that
   follow do you feel you need most?

4. How would your family react if you tried to implement a
   Sabbath? What would you want it to include? Would it be
   different for different members of your family?

5. What one step can you take toward this goal this week?

Chapter 12:
Use the Net; Then Get Up

The Wallendas choose to perform without a net. They believe it keeps them sharp and focused on their precise moves. And they look to God for their protection, not to a net. But it doesn't mean members of the clan haven't fallen, sometimes with fatal results. In 1962, their seven-person pyramid collapsed, killing two family members and paralyzing a third.

I'm thankful I don't have to live life without a net.

I'm not perfect. I won't always be as focused as I should be. When I allow myself to be distracted, I may fall. That's why the safety net exists, and that net is God himself.

Psalm 37 says, "The steps of a man are established by the Lord, and He delights in his way. When he falls, he will not be hurled headlong, because the Lord is the One who holds his hand" (vs. 23–24, NASB). I love that phrase "hurled headlong." Because when I'm pitched off the wire—or to be more accurate, when I step off the wire—God is present. I won't land on my head. He'll catch me. Underneath me will be "the everlasting arms" described in Deuteronomy 33:27. He will be present. He holds my hand.

When I open my eyes as I lie in the net, the first thing I see is the face of Jesus. And he's not there to upbraid me. He holds my hand and looks at me in love. Like a parent bent over a student-athlete who's been injured in a game, he's present to support, to ensure I'm all right, to help me up, and to get me back in the game, back on the wire.

Falls Happen

I'm a faller. I'm not even sure if that's a word, but it's what I am. I trip over everything and nothing. It's so bad I don't go anywhere without my husband telling me to walk carefully.

Once walking into the mall as a youth group chaperone, I caught my toe on something (or nothing) and face planted into the curb. I ripped the knee out of my pants like a six-year-old and cut up my face. Another time I tripped on my own front steps, face first into the concrete and breaking my glasses. Last fall I tripped over a curb headed into The Cheesecake Factory and broke my arm in two places.

When I do tricks like this, first I'm terribly frightened. Then after checking for life-threatening injuries, I'm embarrassed and angry with myself. How can I be so clumsy? What is my problem? How do I stumble over nothing? Why can't I be like normal people and walk without tripping?

The self-recrimination is intense. If I'm alone when I trip, I look around to see if anyone noticed. I don't want to feel like a fool. When I trip but don't fall, I have a standard line I use if someone notices: "Did you see that carpet reach up and grab my foot?" And then I laugh, but I don't think it's funny. I feel foolish.

But I've never yet sat down after a fall and decided then and there never to walk again to prevent falling again. I get up, dust myself off, and move on, albeit a little more carefully, at least for the moment.

And yet when I metaphorically fall—whether through sin like being rude to someone (again) or through inattention to the ways of God so I'm living lazily or crazily rather than purposefully—I often wallow rather than get up. Why is that?

I think it has to do with the voices in my head. When I physically fall, the voice in my head yells, "Get up! Maybe no one has seen you yet." It wants to avoid the embarrassment. It will later berate me for being clumsy or distracted, but by then I'm already moving again.

The Voice in My Head Isn't Mine

I've often heard, and even said in the last chapter, that as Christians, we perform for an audience of one—God the Father. We want to live concerned only about that audience. And yet we need to be aware that another watches who never paid admission to our circus. He snuck in under the side of the tent and for one purpose—to serve as heckler, distractor, and then, when we fall, accuser.

In the book of Job, Satan appears before God and tells him he's come "from roaming through the earth, and going back and forth in it" (1:7). And what is his purpose for roaming the earth? Revelation 12:10 describes him as "the accuser of our brothers, who accuses them before our God day and night."

Satan does his best to distract us on the wire, and when we fall, his is often the first voice we hear. His voice begins while we're still bouncing in the net, trying to catch our breath. He doesn't give us the opportunity to get up and get moving again. He wants us to stay down and out for the rest of the performance.

If the voice in my head is one of condemnation, I'm not hearing the voice of God but, rather, of his mortal enemy.

His is not the loving voice of a parent encouraging us to get up and try again. It's the voice of shame telling us we're useless to God and to everyone else. He tells us we'll never walk the wire successfully, so why not give up now? He reminds us of how much better others are doing up on the wire. He insists we'll never master it like they have, so rather than embarrass the other performers, why don't we just stop attempting to walk the rope.

If the voice in my head is one of condemnation, I'm not hearing the voice of God but, rather, of his mortal enemy. On Twitter the other day I saw this great description on the voice of God versus the voice of the enemy: "Conviction pushes you toward Christ. Condemnation pulls you away from Him. Don't listen to the lies of the enemy. It is not over for you!"[27]

Romans 8:1–2 tells us, "Therefore, there is now no condemnation for those who are in Christ Jesus, because through Christ Jesus the law of the Spirit of life set me free from the law of sin and death." God doesn't condemn us. He already set us free by his Spirit and the work of Christ on the cross.

Brennan Manning, in *The Relentless Tenderness of Jesus*, says, "God loves you as you are and not as you should be!"[28] He goes on to say, "From our brother Jesus, who alone knows the Father, we learn that there is welcoming love, unconditional acceptance, a relentless and eternal affection that so far exceeds our human experience that even the passion and death of Jesus are only a *hint* of it."[29]

God is your biggest cheerleader. When he safely catches you after your misstep off the wire, he treats you with the tenderness of a mother whose child is learning to walk. He picks you up, dusts you off, gives you a kiss, and sends you back up to try again. He may remind you to keep your focus on him because it's the way to find success on the wire, but he never berates you.

Satan's goal in accusing us is to get us to give up, to decide walking the wire with Jesus is undoable. If he can convince me, I'll turn the net into a hammock and get comfortable. I'll lie back and focus on my favorite TV shows. Maybe I'll order in pizza or Chinese. I've become the spectator.

That's one less person choosing to live for Jesus, living to fulfill her purpose. I won't be telling anyone else about the love of Jesus and how he or she can live in it, and so Satan has weakened God's team.

My net hammock might be comfortable for a while, but eventually I'll feel vaguely unsatisfied. The potato chips taste stale. The soda is a bit flat. The TV shows all seem to be reruns. I'm bored. Is this all there is?

Responding to Grace

God smiles. "The wire still waits," he whispers. "Come walk it with me. You can do this." He extends his hand. There's still no condemnation, no "about time" muttered under his breath as I shakily dump myself out of the net and move toward the ladder. Instead he goes with me, encouraging me, reminding me of the gifts of the Spirit he wants me to use as I walk the wire.

"I'll be right out in front of you," he says. "Focus on me. Walk intentionally and be in the moment. Forget this fall. All is forgiven. In fact, it was forgiven thousands of years ago when I died in your place. Let's get back into the performance together."

Satan still yammers in my head. "Don't be a fool. You'll only fall again. And how disappointed God will be with you then." But God is a loving father who's never disappointed with us. He is relentless love. He cheers me on. He tells me I can do it.

When we land with a bounce in the net, we can take a moment to recognize why we ended up here, but then we need to get back on the rope, living the life God imagined for us. If I spend too much time analyzing, inertia sets in. If I spend time berating myself, I'm helping Satan be the accuser by being my own.

I can thank God his forgiveness is true. He's waiting for me

When we fall, God comforts us, catching us in the net woven of his grace and mercy, reaching his hand down to lift us again, giving us a hug as he herds us back up onto the wire.

to walk the wire with him again, and he only wants the best for me.

When the Wallendas' Pyramid of Seven collapsed, Karl Wallenda "managed to grab the wire on his way down and to catch the woman by her hand as she hit him and then fell past him, but his pelvis was cracked and he had a double hernia." Even though he was devastated by the deaths and injuries, Karl "went up on the wire and performed the next day."[30] Within two years the troupe was training to once again perform the Pyramid of Seven, even though "his own daughter ... called him a murderer. But Karl knew ... if they didn't reconstruct the trick ... their lives would have been defined forever by failure and fear."[31]

What failure or fear are you allowing to define your life?

Only allow it to be used by God to shape how he uses you for his kingdom. God is the great recycler—he wastes nothing. He'll take every experience we endure, no matter how painful and no matter how much it was caused by our own foolishness, and redeem it for his kingdom purposes.

Remember how the apostle Paul says it works in 2 Corinthians 1:3–4: "Praise be to the God and Father of our Lord Jesus Christ, the Father of compassion and the God of all comfort, who comforts us in all our troubles, so that we can comfort those in any trouble with the comfort we ourselves have received from God." When we fall, God comforts us, catching us in the net woven of his grace and mercy, reaching his hand down to lift us again, giving us a hug as he herds us back up onto the wire.

He wants us to then repurpose the comfort he gave us to comfort someone else, to help them find restoration back on the wire. Galatians 6, verses 1 and 2, explains how the process should work: "Brothers [and sisters], if someone is caught in a sin, you who are spiritual should restore him gently. But watch yourselves, or you also may be tempted. Carry each other's burdens, and in this way you will fulfill the law of Christ." We reach out a hand; we gently help them reach for God's comfort and wholeness. We take care so we don't fall, which wouldn't help either of us.

In this way we fulfill Christ's command recorded in John 13:34–35: "Love one another. As I have loved you, so you must love one another. By this all men will know that you are my disciples, if you love one another." When we provide comfort and restoration to others we're living the love of Christ and the world will recognize us as followers of Christ.

How many times have you heard someone say, "The church is the only army that shoots its wounded"? It may have become a cliché, but the sad truth behind it remains. We often destroy those who fall off the wire by heaping condemnation on them. When we do this, we're living as instruments of Satan, not as instruments of righteousness.

God's plan is always restoration. In his sermon yesterday on the woman caught in adultery (John 8), my husband Les said, "Where Jesus is present, grace prevails." When we allow Jesus to be present in and through us, grace will prevail in bringing others back to wholeness, back up onto the wire to begin again. Help them to focus on Jesus, not you, but be the hand of grace to get them to that place.

When we fall—and we will—we give thanks for the mercy of God that catches us and the grace of God that restores us back to the wire. We ask the Spirit of God to help us tune out the voice of accuser in our heads and hearts and to focus on the loving face of Jesus out in front, ready to keep us moving on the wire of his purpose. And we, like Karl Wallenda, reach out and grab those who are falling past us on their way down.

The net exists for our protection, but it's never meant to be where we live. Get up, and get back onto that wire, finding the balance God has for you.

Questions for Contemplation or Discussion

1. When you take a misstep in your life, what are your first thoughts? Do you condemn yourself or remind yourself to turn to God and his grace?

2. What have you tried to do and failed at? Did you ever try again? Why or why not?

3. What are the ways Satan accuses you of not being the Christian you should be? How can you combat his voice of accusation with the promises of God?

4. Is there something God has called you to do that previous failure(s) have caused you to give up on? What kind of support could you seek out from others so you can begin again?

5. As you think of the tightrope walker, what one action step could you take this week to begin to move your life further into balance?

Conclusion:
Make Your Circus "The Greatest Show On Earth"

P. T. Barnum began billing his show as "The Greatest Show On Earth" back in the 1870s. Ringling Brothers and Barnum & Bailey continues to refer to its circus this way more than 140 years later.

Unfortunately, my life circus doesn't even feel like a mediocre show most days, let alone a great one.

If we're thinking in the spiritual realm, though, I think most of us would be quick to call the life of Jesus "the greatest show on earth." After all, he came to show us what it would look like if God moved in next door. He was fully man, but also fully God, and it showed in the way he lived his life.

He performed amazing healings, from blindness and mental illness, and he raised people from the dead. He challenged the status quo and didn't look to associate with the powerful, but instead he hung out with the outcasts, revealing the love of God to them.

And in the greatest show of love ever, he died on a cruel cross to pay for sin he didn't commit. He was able to pay for my sin and yours, sins that wouldn't even be committed for more than 2,000 years. What an awesome feat!

But Jesus didn't think his "show" was the greatest show on earth. In John 14:10, Jesus credits his amazing work, not to himself, but to the Father: "The words I say to you are not just my own. Rather, it is the Father, living in me, who's doing his work." Then he goes on to say, in essence, "But wait; you ain't seen nothin' yet." Listen to verse 12: "I tell you the truth, anyone who has faith in me will do what I have been doing. *He will do even greater things than these*, because I am going to the Father" (emphasis added).

We—you and I—will do greater works than Jesus? That seems totally impossible. How can we possibly beat that show? Jesus was God! I'm not. Are you?

And yet, God lives within us. The Father, who was "doing his work" in Jesus, has sent his Spirit to live within each person who accepts what Jesus did on the cross was for her benefit. When people invite him into their lives and begin a relationship with God, the Spirit moves in. We become children of God.

First John 3:1–2 describes who we are and what it means for our lives:

> How great is the love the Father has lavished on us, that we should be called children of God! And that is what we are! …
> Dear friends, now we are children of God, and what we will be has not yet been made known. But we know that when he appears, we shall be like him, for we shall see him as he is.

Someday we will be exactly like Jesus. We're not there yet, but we already have all of the power of God living within us, able to do the work of God in and through our lives. And millions of us walk this earth today. So rather than just one Jesus in one place, with the Father working through him, God now has millions of Christians across the globe, all able to do the work of God at the same time in every place.

Like the genie in *Aladdin*, we've all got "phenomenal cosmic powers" in an "itty-bitty living space." The earth-forming, miracle-working, always-loving power of the God of the universe resides in my body and yours.

If I allow him to work, what might he be able to do? If every Christian gave God free reign to work from within his or her body and mind and heart, how would the world change?

Focusing on Jesus, so I open my life and heart to his direction, is the only way to allow the Spirit of God to do the Father's work in me. He can transform my daily circus from chaos into the greatest show on earth, bringing glory to the Father.

Jesus once told the Jewish leaders: "I tell you the truth, the Son can do nothing by himself; he can do only what he sees his Father doing, because whatever the Father does the Son also does" (John 5:19). If I'm going to live purposefully in my life, I need to stop and see what God is doing and, through the power of his Spirit, do that as well. To paraphrase Henry Blackaby in *Experiencing God*, "we must find what God is doing and join him there."

Someday we will be exactly like Jesus. We're not there yet, but we already have all of the power of God living within us, able to do the work of God in and through our lives.

Another verse, a prayer really, from *The Message* has become my tightrope-walking reminder. It comes from the blessing King Solomon spoke over the people of Israel as they dedicated the temple of God:

> May he keep us centered and devoted to him,
> following the life path he has cleared,
> watching the signposts,
> walking at the pace and rhythm he laid down
> (1 Kings 8:58).

I love that the verse says God's cleared the path already. I make my life difficult. I build my own roadblocks of false expectations, and throw the debris of the inconsequential on the path, which I then stumble over. I get so much more done if I stop and consult God first, hearing his heart for my day. And the bonus is it's productive work; it includes kingdom-of-God work, actions that impact eternity.

God gives me signposts, if I'll only slow down and watch for them. He doesn't want my life to be chaotic and confusing. But my mind and fears and plans are often so far ahead of where I am on the path that I miss the signposts in place for today. Slowing down, consulting God, and remembering my purpose bring me back to the present where I can notice the instructions he's trying to give me.

And how beautiful to think of "the pace and rhythm he laid down." Not the pace I lay down, whether pushing myself to the point of exhaustion or wallowing in laziness and self-indulgence. It's also not the pace my husband lays down. I've spent 35 years trying to keep up with my husband Les. I couldn't do it back in college when I took naps every afternoon in an attempt to keep going as long into the evening as he did. I certainly can't do it now. And the pace isn't even the one my friends or ministry leaders lay down.

It's the pace and rhythm the God who created me and knows me best lays down just for me. It works for me because my designer designed it. And it will be the perfect pace to enjoy the life God has for me while I fulfill the purpose he has for me.

We only get the clear path, the obvious signposts, and the proper pace, though, if we remain "centered and devoted to him." Stay on the wire, with our eyes fixed on Jesus. He is the key to balance in the circus of life.

Are you discovering his rhythm, his grace, his pace?

Acknowledgements

This book would never have happened if it had not been for the untold number of women who, after hearing me speak on *Finding Balance in the Circus of Life*, said to me, "You need to write this as a book!" As you can see, you finally wore me down. Thank you.

I'm grateful for the meeting and retreat planners who've invited me to speak on balance to your groups. I love your enthusiasm and creativity for the topic—in decorations, food, and fun. You rock!

Many fellow writers and dear friends have encouraged me, pushed me, prodded me, cheered me on, edited me, prayed for me, counseled me, and loved me through this process. I am eternally grateful to God for bringing you into my life. Special shout-outs to Lisa Bartelt, Mandy Bell, Stephanie Giles, Mary Grossman, Cathy Jennings, Margie Miller, and Rochelle Owens for not only believing I could do this but also ensuring I did.

Jaime Scott, thank you for allowing me to use your wonderfully quirky *Little Tightrope Walker* illustration for both my speaking engagements and this book's front cover. I love it, and appreciate your generosity. And Tino Wallenda, I'm so glad I discovered your book *Walking the Straight and Narrow* all those years ago. It enriched this book and the talks I've done on balance over the years. Thank you for allowing me to quote it in *Finding Balance in the Circus of Life*.

Les, you make my writing and speaking life happen by taking on so many tasks I don't get around to. And you do it with grace and with pride in what God is calling me to do. You are an amazing gift of God in my life—and funny too. Thanks, Bookend, for all you do and even more for all you are.

God has allowed me to do work I love. I'm so thankful. May this book bring glory to him.

About the Author

Carol Cool is a speaker, blogger, and writer who loves to help her audiences discover their God-created uniqueness so they live authentically and joyfully. She encourages average people like herself to make a difference in their world by living out the gifts and purpose God implanted within them. Carol has served with her husband Rev. Leslie Cool in youth work, church planting, and church ministry. She loves good books, good food, and Panera Bread (sometimes all at once).

Visit her on Facebook or on her website:
 www.carolcool.com
 www.facebook.com/carolrcool/

Notes

[1] "Iverson Breaks Ground as Circus Ringmaster," *Technique*, the newspaper of Georgia Tech, February 15, 2002, pp. 17–18.

[2] Quotes on Gunther Gebel-Williams are taken from the program book for the 119th edition of "The Greatest Show On Earth," and other pages that previously appeared on the ringling.com website. Author retains copies of the site.

[3] www.charliethejugglingclown.com/definition.htm

[4] Wallis, Claudia and Steptoe, Sonja, *Time Magazine,* January 16, 2006, p. 75.

[5] Ibid.

[6] Wainwright, Martin, *The Guardian*, April 21, 2005; www.guardian.co.uk/technology/2005/apr/22/money.workandcareers

[7] Beek, Peter J. and Lewbel, Arthur, *Scientific American*, November 1995, Volume 273, Number 5, pp. 92–97; https://www2.bc.edu/~lewbel/jugweb/science-1.html

[8] Wallace, Kelly, "Sorry to Ask But ... Do Women Apologize More Than Men?", CNN, www.cnn.com/2014/06/26/living/women-apologize-sorry-pantene-parents/, June 26, 2014.

[9] McGee, Robert S., *The Search for Significance*, Thomas Nelson, 2003, pp. 7–10.

[10] Graf, Jonathan, *Praying Like Paul*, PrayerShop Publishing, 2008, p. 10.

[11] McGinnis, Ruth, *Breathing Freely,* Fleming H. Revell, 2002, pp. 20–22.

[12] Wallenda, Tino, *Walking the Straight and Narrow*, Bridge-Logos, 2005, pp. 97–98.

[13] Ibid., p. xi.

[14] Ibid., p. 100.

[15] Taken from the Curious Gibberish website at www.curiousgibberish.com/are-you-starting-to-notice-that-new-car-you-just-bought-your-ras-system-has-activated/, which is no longer active. Author retains copy of site.

[16] All non-Scripture quotes in the following paragraphs on SHAPE are taken from Rick Warren's book *The Purpose Driven Life*, pp. 236–255.

[17] www.youtube.com/watch?v=gHzrfVJYHSI&list=UURk7mQqlWLqd36kqFjeAWGw&index=9

[18] Wallenda, Tino, *Walking the Straight and Narrow*, Bridge-Logos, 2005, p. 116.

[19] McGinnis, Ruth, *Breathing Freely,* Fleming H. Revell, 2002, pp. 20–21.

[20] Wallenda, Tino, *Walking the Straight and Narrow*, Bridge-Logos, 2005, p. 118.

[21] McGinnis, Ruth, *Breathing Freely,* Fleming H. Revell, 2002, pp. 20–21.

[22] Higginbotham, Adam, "Touching the Void," *The Guardian*, January 18, 2003, www.guardian.co.uk/theobserver/2003/jan/19/features.magazine57

[23] Wallenda, Tino, *Walking the Straight and Narrow*, Bridge-Logos, 2005, p. 103.

[24] Ibid., pp. 92, 127.

[25] Ibid., p. 87.

[26] Lopatto, Elizabeth, "Poor Sleep Alters Genes, Raises Risk of Disease," *Intelligencer Journal/Lancaster New Era*, February 27, 2013, no longer available online. Author retains copy of article.

[27] Caine, Christine (@ChristineCaine), 4/2/13, 1:35 PM.

[28] Manning, Brennan, *The Relentless Tenderness of Jesus*, Revell, 2004, p. 25.

[29] Ibid., p. 138.

[30] Wallenda, Tino, *Walking the Straight and Narrow*, Bridge-Logos, 2005, p. 112.

[31] Ibid., p. 113.

CPSIA information can be obtained at www.ICGtesting.com
Printed in the USA
BVOW04s0848060916

461037BV00001B/2/P